The Love Deal

MISHA BELL

♠ MOZAIKA PUBLICATIONS ♠

Copyright © 2023 Misha Bell
www.mishabell.com

Published by Mozaika Publications, an imprint of Mozaika LLC.
www.mozaikallc.com

Cover by Najla Qamber Designs
www.qamberdesignsmedia.com

ISBN: 978-1-63142-797-8
Paperback ISBN: 978-1-63142-798-5

One

"BUNNY, STOP FUCKING YOUR SISTER!"

I accompany my words with the "shoo" gesture I use when I catch him on my pillow.

The evil cat doesn't even acknowledge my presence.

Pearl examines the feline lovers with a grin that's identical to mine, right down to the crinkles around her green eyes. "His sister?" she says skeptically. "Unlike us, these two aren't from the same litter."

I glower at her. "Use logic. Bunny is my fur baby, and Atonic is yours—ergo, siblings."

Pearl and I are two of six identical sisters, a.k.a. sextuplets. Some of us call ourselves a "litter," though I prefer the term "clutch."

She snorts. "Wouldn't our kids be cousins?"

Shit. She's right, but who admits such things to the members of one's clutch? Instead, I channel Pixie, another clutch mate. "Since you and I share the same

1

DNA, our kids from different fathers would be biological half-siblings."

Pixie is obsessed with identical multiples like us and has recently not-so-jokingly suggested that we should all reproduce with a group of identical sextuplet males so that "all our kids would be DNA brothers and sisters."

Pearl gives me an exasperated look. "Oh, come on. No matter how alike your personalities, you don't share any DNA with your psycho cat."

Would it help my case if I informed Pearl that humans share ninety percent of their DNA with cats? Probably not.

"How are our personalities alike?" I ask instead.

"You know how," Pearl says. "In any case, all of this is moot. Cats don't have an incest taboo and will gladly inbreed when given the chance."

That last bit doesn't deserve a reply, so I look back at my living room carpet, where the action is still going on. "Isn't that adorable... in a messed-up sort of way?"

I blame said adorableness on the out-of-control cuteness of our cats. Bunny is a Japanese Bobtail, which means he has a tiny tail reminiscent of his namesake's —a bunny. His fur is white with some black patches on his face that make him look equally like a raccoon, a panda, and a bandit. Atonic, my sister's cat, is a blue-eyed Himalayan with a flat face that wears a perpetually sleepy expression.

Pearl's lips quirk. "I bet any furry creature clumsily

mounting another would be adorable, be it an Ewok, a Wookie, or whatever Cousin Itt is."

I peer at the cats more closely. My normally graceful cat does look really clumsy doing this. Wait… "What's he doing?"

What he's doing is biting poor Atonic's neck, I realize, which eerily fits the running joke about Bunny being a psychopathic killer. Psychopaths bite women's necks when they have coitus, right? Or is that vampires?

"That's typical," Pearl says. "The tomcat will grab the scruff of the queen's neck with his teeth while mating."

Huh. Is someone purring now? I tear my eyes away from the cats and look at my sister quizzically. "How do you know so much about cat reproduction?"

She shrugs. "Before I found my calling, I thought about becoming a cat breeder."

"This show would've been a regular Monday for you then." I nod at the busy cats. "Making cheese doesn't sound so funny in comparison."

"Har har."

"Sorry," I say. "Was that joke too cheesy?"

Pearl opens her mouth, undoubtedly to unleash a scathing retort, but at that very moment, the gates of Hell open. Or so I assume because the blood-chilling, panty-soiling howl/shriek that comes out of her cat is like all the demons in Hell screaming at once. No. Make that shapeshifting banshees who turn into pigs on a full moon—and get stuck with dull knives.

It's official. After years of "my cat is a serial killer" jokes, Bunny has gone ahead and become one, and now he's torture-killing my sister's poor cat.

I leap forward to stop whatever this is, but Pearl grabs my elbow. "Don't! That's normal."

I make sure Pearl hasn't sprouted horns, nor is otherwise showing signs of having been replaced with a demon from that open gate to Hell. "How could something that sounds like that be normal?"

"A tomcat's penis has barbs," she says. "When he pulls out, it hurts the queen, and she caterwauls."

Oh, no. I keep my eyes away from her cat's vagina, in case there's blood. Blood and I do not mix, at all. I faint at the sight of it, or worse. But hey, at least I won't ever, under any circumstances, fall for a vampire, no matter how sparkly.

Regardless, the last thing I need is for Pearl to notice my reaction and blab to the rest of the family. It's bad enough that one of my sisters already suspects something. Over the years, I've cultivated a reputation as "the tough sextuplet," in part to hide my weakness. After all, could someone afraid of blood get as many tattoos or piercings as I have? The answer is obviously yes. It wasn't easy, and I did swoon a number of times at the tattoo parlor, but I blamed it on dehydration and low blood sugar.

Suddenly, Bunny leaps away from Atonic—and just in time. She's stopped caterwauling and is trying to smack him in the furry face with her unsheathed claws.

He gives me an uncharacteristically frightened

stare, and I can't help but picture what he'd say if he had the equipment to do so:

It-that-feeds-me has to help. I've tortured and killed one victim too many and now face the cat version of Dexter.

Meanwhile, Atonic rolls on the floor a few times, then viciously hisses at Bunny.

"Maybe we should separate them?" Pearl asks.

"You think?" I grab Bunny off the floor. "It probably would've been a good idea to separate them this morning, when the two of you arrived."

Or here's an idea: she could have left her cat back in Los Angeles. Her excuse for not doing so was pretty flimsy—something about her best friend's boyfriend being allergic to cats.

Pearl carefully approaches her own cat. "That or fix them, despite propaganda from Mom and Dad."

I wince. Our parents firmly believe in reproductive freedom for all living beings, including pets and every rescued animal that lives on their farm. Their propaganda must have sunk in deep for me because I didn't even think about neutering Bunny before Pearl said this.

Taking Bunny to my bedroom, I set him on my pillow—the only way he'll tolerate the indignity I've just submitted him to. At least without gouging out my eyes.

"Stay," I tell him sternly and lock the door behind me.

When I come back to the living room, Pearl has not

only caught her charge but has managed to soothe her a bit.

"Well," I say, brushing cat hair off my leather jacket. "That happened."

She sighs. "We'll have to keep them apart for about three days, or else they'll do more of that."

"More?" I gape at her cat. "Didn't I just hear the words 'penis' and 'barbs' in the same sentence?"

Pearl shrugs. "Doesn't matter. That pain started her ovulation cycle."

I shudder. "I never thought I'd say this, but I'm glad I'm not a cat."

Just as Pearl starts to reply, I'm startled yet again by a vigorous knocking on my front door.

Strange. I'm not expecting any deliveries or visitors.

I rush over. "Who is it?"

"The police," says a gruff voice. "Open up."

Two

THE POLICE? WHAT THE HELL?

Heart thumping, I check the peephole.

Yep. They're dressed like cops.

Did a neighbor call them because of the caterwauling? It did sound like bloody murder. But how did they get here so fast? Unless…

Fuck. It can't be about the coupons again, can it?

"Open the door, or we'll be forced to open it," a hard-faced cop says.

Well, shit. I can't afford to repair this door.

There's no choice.

I open the door.

The cop looks from me to Pearl. "Honey Hyman?"

"That's me." And yes, I know my name sounds like a virginal membrane that people with diabetes should avoid.

"You're under arrest," he informs me. "For fraud."

My stomach drops. I turn to Pearl, who is as pale as

the ghost of a toilet. My voice is strained as I say, "Let Blue know, okay?"

Blue is our clutch mate who used to work for the government, so if anyone can help with this, it would be her.

The rest is like a nightmare. I'm led out of the building, put in a police car, brought unceremoniously into the station, and shepherded into a room—all the while fielding a surge of adrenaline so strong I barely register any of it.

Did someone read me my Miranda Rights? If not, do I get a refund?

They didn't take my butterfly knife, which is weird because I always thought going to jail was like flying on a plane—weapons aren't allowed.

Maybe I'm not going to jail? Dare I hope?

I think back on the last two times I was in trouble. Both were actually interrelated situations.

First, there was Tiffany, a cheerleader who bullied me for ogling her uber-hot boyfriend, Gunther— something I *was* guilty of. Eventually, I stood up to her with a knife—only as a threat, though, since the last thing I wanted was to draw any blood. Unfortunately, the dumdum didn't notice said knife and got up in my face anyway, accidentally slicing her arm open. To this day, I don't know how bad the cut was, as I couldn't look at the wound on account of the blood. Since Tiffany didn't end up with a scar, I imagine the cut wasn't so bad—not that it helped me escape the resulting suspension and mark on my permanent record. On the bright side, that incident is what started my "don't mess with me" reputation, which I don't mind at all, as it has kept the other Tiffanies of the world away.

The second incident took place a year later, still in high school. It involved Gunther again—who was no longer with Tiffany at the time. Not that I kept track. Much. That time, not only did I get suspended and *really* tarnish my permanent record, but I also barely dodged the juvenile justice system.

It all started when I was little. For whatever reason, I became obsessed with all things saving money, including deals and coupons. After taking an art class my junior year, I realized that tweaking percentages on coupons with a white pen was just as profitable as counterfeiting money—so I did it, first for myself and then for the other kids at my school. As it turned out, one of the stores that lost money because of my creative initiative was owned by Gunther's family, so when Gunther learned of my activities, he tattled to the principal. Shit hit the fan, and I'm paying for it to this day.

My phone rings.

Huh. Another thing they didn't take.

I check it.

It's Blue. Good. Pearl must've told her to get in touch.

"Hi," I say, switching to a form of Pig Latin Blue developed when we were kids. "Let's talk quick. They might come back and take my phone."

"The quick version is, whatever they have against you is physical, not digital, so there's not much I can do here," Blue says.

Blue hasn't had any trouble with the law, but she doesn't seem to have much respect for certain legalities after working for—as she calls it—"No Such Agency." Case in point: she's just admitted to hacking into the police department's computers as casually as I'd admit to watching cat videos on TikTok.

"Can your former colleagues help?" I ask.

"Sorry, no," she says. "I know some feds, but that doesn't help your case. If you want, I can text you the name of an excellent lawyer."

"Sure." Except I have no idea how I'd pay said lawyer. Thanks to my high school mishaps, no college wanted me, and I never achieved my dream of becoming a wealthy business owner. Currently, I work part-time sweeping floors at a tattoo parlor and cutting hair at a barbershop.

"I can lend you some money," Blue says, clearly reading my mind.

"No." I hate charity. "I'll take the public attorney."

"It's coupons again, isn't it?" she whispers.

"I'm not sure I should talk about it," I whisper back. "Even in code."

I hear her type a few keystrokes. Then she whispers, "You don't need to say anything. I just checked, and the answer is yes."

Fuck. I want to smack myself. After years of walking the straight and narrow, I got tempted to play

Robin Hood, and this is the result. My neighborhood family-owned grocery store was recently replaced by the uber-expensive Munch & Crunch supermarket, and my elderly neighbors told me that they're struggling to afford food. So I fudged a few coupons for them. Why is that even a crime?

"Someone is coming your way," Blue says, startling me out of my reverie. "Talk later."

Before I can wonder how she knows that, she hangs up and the door opens.

I gape at the man who walks in. The epitome of tall, dark, and handsome, he has neatly cut, smoothed-back brown hair that makes me think of corporate boardrooms and OCD. His strong chin and muscular jaw are clean-shaven to the point of shine, and his eyes, a vivid emerald-green two shades brighter than mine, are narrowed with disapproval, his full lips pursed tight.

Who is he, and why does he look familiar?

In that perfectly tailored suit, he's unlikely to be a cop. Perhaps a lawyer that I can't afford? It's possible, but there's something annoyingly honest and noble in his features that I associate more with Boy Scouts than with ambulance chasers.

"Honey Hyman," he says with distaste—and shock rolls through me as I recognize his deliciously deep baritone, one he's had since his teenage years.

"Gunther Ferguson?" I blurt incredulously.

Is it possible that I conjured him up by thinking of him on the way here, kind of like invoking a demon?

Or maybe I fell asleep in the police car and I'm dreaming?

If not, then this man is what happened to the boy I hate, the one who got me into trouble in high school, thus proving that karma is a fucking myth. If there were any justice in the world, he would've grown warped and deformed with time, like an evil lord of the Sith, but the opposite has happened.

Like an Anne Rice vampire, the evil transformation has made him hotter.

"Is playing dumb your latest game?" Gunther pulls out a stack of coupons and tosses them on the table. "Are you going to pretend you didn't know that it's my store you've been stealing from?"

Stunned, I glance down.

Yep. Those expertly faked coupons are for that small-business-crushing Munch & Crunch. And indeed, they are my handywork—but that store is part of a multinational chain of supermarkets, so how can it be his? Unless...

"You own that Munch & Crunch, like a franchise?" I ask stupidly.

He scoffs. "I own the whole company. Like you didn't know that."

I blink. "How would I know that?"

He gestures at the coupons. "The same way you know how to make those look indistinguishable from the real thing."

Hold on. Is he just a clever cop? "I'm not about to incriminate myself. Assuming those are actually fake,

I'm sure whoever created them did it to help out their elderly neighbors who used to shop at the place that your Munch & Crunch ruthlessly drove out of business. Those folks can't afford your regular prices. In any case, how could that mystery person know that you had anything to do with the store? I know the likes of you think you're the center of the universe, but that's just not true."

He sighs. "First, you did this same thing to my dad. Now me. If this isn't targeted, I have to assume you make so many fraudulent coupons that this has inexorably happened again."

I push the coupons away. "Not admitting anything —but what about bad luck?"

His full lips curl in a sneer. "I don't believe in luck."

"Oh, luck exists." Bad luck is the only thing that can explain how tempting his mouth looks—despite what it's saying.

"You can prevaricate as much as you want, but the case against you is airtight. In fact, I've been led to believe you'll face jail this time. Unless…"

Wait. Is this blackmail? "Unless what?"

A dozen naughty scenarios of what he might demand of me play out in my mind—some involving handcuffs (because police station), others candle wax (no idea why), and a bunch more featuring a bed covered in BOGO coupons.

His green eyes gleam triumphantly. "Unless you work for me. Then I'll drop the charges."

Three

"Excuse me?" Did he say work *for* or *under*?

He pulls out a paper and slaps it on the desk in front of me. "That's your contract. It states that you'll Honey-proof my coupons—both digital and physical."

I snatch the document without looking. "Why?"

He arches a dark eyebrow. "It's like in *Catch Me If You Can.* Who could do this better than the scammer queen herself?"

The negative connotation of "scammer" aside, I don't want to be called a queen either—not after the way Pearl used that word in the context of cat reproduction.

Tearing my eyes away from my nemesis's annoyingly symmetrical features, I scan the document. The legalese does seem to say something along the lines of what he stated.

My phone dings.

It's a text from Blue.

Take the deal.

How did she…? Never mind. Blue's nickname should be Big Brother—or Equal-Sized Sister—because she's always watching.

"Are you really on your phone in the middle of this?" Gunther's voice holds a distinct edge.

I look up at him. "How long is this arrangement for?" I ask, ignoring the question.

He sits in the chair opposite mine. "Until the work is done."

"What's my rate?" I ask.

He names a number.

I nearly fall off my chair.

"It's non-negotiable," he says, misreading my expression.

Damn. Given how broke I am, he didn't need to blackmail me. He could've just offered me this money.

Well, maybe not. It's not quite "work for someone you hate" kind of money—but it's close.

My phone dings again.

Knowing it'll piss him off, I pointedly have a look at the screen.

If you want something to negotiate with, tell him you know he's been stalking you on social media. For years.

Stalking me? For years? Why?

Then it hits me. He's been plotting revenge—for me cutting his girlfriend and for the fake coupons to his father's store. If true, and my working for him *is* the revenge, he will make sure I'll hate it as much as I hate him—so, a lot.

When I meet his gaze again, he's full-on scowling. "So?" he growls. "Have you decided?"

"Yes. No."

His chiseled jaw twitches. "Which is it?"

"*Yes*, I have decided, and *no* is my answer," I say. "My whole life I've lived by a policy that if compensation isn't negotiable, I refuse to consider it."

This is just like bargaining for the right prices at brick-and-mortar stores—something I live for.

"Fine." He rises to his feet—and my heart sinks as I envision the unspeakable acts I might be forced to perform in jail as someone's bitch… all because of my deal addiction.

I'm about to tell him I've reconsidered when he says, "I'll give you one chance to counter."

Shocked, I name a number that tops his by ten percent—conservative because if this were a real job negotiation, I would've gone with twenty.

Blue texts me instantly, and this time, I make sure he doesn't see me sneak a peek.

Ballsy. I'm not sure if I'm proud of you or worried about your sanity.

Gunther takes out a fancy-looking pen and slides it my way. "It's a deal if you sign in the next two minutes."

I scan the contract again, making sure I'm not giving him my firstborn or my soul. It looks legit. With a reluctant sigh, I sign the damn thing.

He picks it up and slaps a business card on the table in front of me. "Be there tomorrow for your first day."

He turns to leave, then over his shoulder adds, "I'll let them know I'm dropping the charges."

I nod, but he's already gone.

I sit there, stunned. Before I can fully process what's just happened, I'm released and delivered home in a police car.

Four

"TELL ME EVERYTHING," PEARL DEMANDS AS I STEP INTO my apartment.

I fully expected the interrogation. Pearl is the biggest gossip in our gossipy family.

We sit on the living room couch, Pearl with her cat in her lap and me with a bottle of soda that I bought for ten cents—thanks to legit couponing. As I tell her what happened, her eyes grow so big she reminds me of an anime character.

"Why do you think he offered you the job?" she asks when I finish.

I shrug. "Probably because of what he said. He needs to secure his coupons."

My sister cocks her head. "Are you sure it's not because he likes you?"

Likes me? "Are you insane?"

She strokes her sleeping cat thoughtfully. "There's got to be other coupon experts in the world."

I sip my soda. "He probably wants to kill two birds —torment me *and* secure his coupons."

"Maybe. But if it's because he wants you, what will you do?"

I scoff. "He doesn't."

She gives me a look eerily reminiscent of our mom's. "You've been single for too long."

"Like you've dated much."

"I don't have a hot guy from high school available," she says. "A guy who definitely used to stare at you in the cafeteria."

My heart skips a beat. "He did?"

She nods.

"No way. How would he even know which one I was? I sat with five identical-to-me people." When it comes to the tattoos and piercings that distinguish me currently, I only had a few back then, and in hidden places—so *that* wouldn't have helped Gunther in the slightest.

Pearl chuckles. "Don't you always claim you're the most attractive of the six of us?"

"Because I am," I say confidently—and wish I could believe it. Statements like that are what I started saying after I read *The Secret*. I figured that if the law of attraction is real, then maybe I could manifest outstanding looks for myself—which would be an amazing deal, like that time I got Dad a set of tires free of charge, and then got three hundred bucks for myself after rebate. Shrugging off the memory, I continue. "In any case, I doubt he could tell who was the most attractive of us from a distance."

Pearl rolls her eyes. "Have you already forgotten your green-hair phase? Or how early your leather-wearing began?"

Shit. She's right. Now that I think about it, the last time I had the traumatic experience of being mistaken for one of my sisters was back in middle school.

"It's all moot anyway," I say firmly. "Even if I wanted to date—which I don't—Gunther would be the last guy I'd consider. I hate him for ruining my life. And he hates me for cutting Tiffany and for the coupons crap. And besides, we're just too different. He's polished, and I'm anything but. He's rich, I'm poor. He's a—"

"The lady doth protest too much," Pearl says conspiratorially to her cat. "Methinks."

"Shut up."

"Well…" She grins impishly. "You have to admit, you've given the date-Gunther idea a whole lot of thought."

"Have not."

"Have too."

"Nuh-uh."

"Uh-huh."

We continue like that for a while until she capitulates by saying, "I believe I've made my point."

I glance pointedly at her cat. "Do you think Atonic is preggers?"

Pearl shrugs. "Not guaranteed, but if we stay here with you, she'll be for sure, and with a big litter at that."

"Even if I lock Bunny away from her?"

"Life will find a way," Pearl says in her best Jeff Goldblum impersonation. "Just like with you and Gunther."

Not wanting to revisit our sophisticated debate from a minute ago, I say, "So where will you stay, if not with me?"

"With Pixie," she says.

"Why?"

She looks down at her cat. "Blue also has a tomcat, Lemon got herself a very edible rodent, Olive is in Florida now, Gia—"

"What about Pixie's giant turtle?"

She sighs. "It's still the best of all the possible scenarios. I doubt I'll find a hotel that allows pets."

"Okay," I say. "When you're ready, I'll help you pack."

———

After Pearl departs, I let Bunny out of the bedroom.

Looking indignant, he beelines for the kitchen and angrily crunches the kibble I got him on a BOGO deal.

"Sorry," I say to him. "Had to wait until Atonic left."

He looks up at me with his usual murderous expression:

So I don't get to torture-murder a member of my own species? How disappointing. It-that-feeds-me had better sleep lightly as it might wake up to a claw—or a fang—gouging out its eye.

When Bunny loses interest in me (a millisecond later), I tell him that I love him, then start preparing for the upcoming workday—a task that consists of a question I never thought I'd ask myself because it goes against my very nature.

How would one thwart a faux coupon?

Five

MUNCH & CRUNCH CORPORATE HEADQUARTERS ARE IN Midtown, so I have to suffer through the indignity that is the morning commute in NYC. Not surprisingly, my destination turns out to be a skyscraper. According to the plaques, Munch & Crunch doesn't occupy the whole building, only a chunk of it.

A crunchy chunk?

"Honey?" the security lady asks with a grin. "People must call you *hon* all the time."

"Not if they don't like getting knifed in the spleen," I reply, keeping my tone jovial but my eyes dead serious.

Might as well let my usual reputation spread at my new workplace.

Her grin replaced with a more professional expression, she tells me I'm to head up to the executive suites on the top floor.

That's odd. I wonder why Gunther wants me there?

When I get to my floor, a heavyset man greets me.

His suit looks baggy on him, his hair is almost nonexistent, and his round face reminds me of a cherub.

"Ms. Hyman?" he asks in a surprisingly warm tone.

"Please, call me Honey," I say. "And never, ever, call me Hon."

A smile lifts his chubby cheeks. "In that case, call me Ashildr, and never, ever call me Ash."

I shake his hand. "Where do I sit?"

He blushes. "That is still being worked out. In the meantime, would you like a tour?"

"If I'm already on the clock, sure."

He grins. "How about we start at the pantry?"

I let him lead me down the hall. We pass a stylishly dressed lady. When she's out of earshot, Ashildr whispers, "That's Linda. Mr. Ferguson hired her as a favor to a business associate. She's friendly enough but will talk about you behind your back."

I arch an eyebrow. "Talk behind your back?"

Was Ashildr's sense of irony surgically removed? Next thing you know, he'll call the next person we meet the office gossip.

"There," he says, and we step into a room the size of my living room.

"You call this a pantry?" I scan a sleek, industrial-sized coffee maker, a restaurant-style fridge, a giant bowl with various fruits, and an obscene assortment of snacks sprawled over every surface. "This is more like a kitchen. At a catering hall."

He grabs a cup and presses a button on the coffee

maker. "Mr. Ferguson doesn't like the term 'breakroom.' He thinks that encourages too many unnecessary breaks." He points at the sign above the microwave. "Speaking of Mr. Ferguson, this notice is from him, which makes it *the law*."

No fish. No popcorn. No curry.

"Huh," I say. "Is Gunther sensitive to smells?"

My clutch mate Lemon has an extreme version of this, to the point where I have to use unscented products for two days before seeing her, or else listen to endless complaints.

"Please call him Mr. Ferguson," Ashildr says pointedly. "And he's not sensitive, just considerate of everyone's sanity."

We'll see. I'm suddenly developing a craving for a fish curry with caramel popcorn for dessert.

Ashildr spreads his arms like he's asking for an ovation. "Do you want to get any snacks or make a drink before we continue the tour?"

I feel a familiar deal-related dopamine rush. "It's all free, right?"

"Of course."

I grab a handful of raspberries. "Are they washed?"

He nods, so I stuff the berries into my mouth. As I chew, I grab three candy bars and stick them into the pockets of my leather jacket. Then I grab a muffin and two nectarines.

Ashildr looks at me with a confused expression. "If you're hungry, I'll take you to the cafeteria."

I swallow my mouthful. "Is the cafeteria free?"

"No, but it's heavily subsidized."

"No, thanks." I eye a second muffin. "I'm good."

"How about I show you the gym?" he asks, following my gaze.

I narrow my eyes. "What are you implying?"

Ashildr pales. "I just figured that since you're interested in the free perks, you might—"

"I was just fucking with you," I say with a grin.

"Please refrain from using the f-word," he says with a cringe. "Especially around Mr. Ferguson."

"Noted," I say, fighting the urge to grin evilly. "Go ahead, take me to the gym."

"Sure." Ashildr eyes my hands with disapproval.

I sigh and grudgingly put back one of the nectarines. "Let's go."

Just as he turns to go, a woman steps into the room —a coolly beautiful blonde who appears vaguely familiar. Ignoring Ashildr, she looks me up and down, like a museum exhibit.

"Do we know each other?" she asks, perfect nose crinkling.

"This is Ms. Hyman," Ashildr says and turns to me. "This is Ms. Ichor."

I blink. I knew someone with that exact last name in high school. Her name was Tiffany—the very same Tiffany Gunther used to date.

As in, the bully who cut herself on my knife.

A spark of recognition is already in her eyes, followed by hatred, of course.

"What are you doing here?" she hisses at me.

"She's a new hire," Ashildr explains, looking rather taken aback at her tone. "I believe you're working together."

"We are?" Tiffany and I shout in unison.

He blanches. "I'm sure Mr. Ferguson will tell you all about it later today."

So, this is Gunther's wicked plan—to make me work with the worst person in the world? Besides him, that is.

With a sniff, Tiffany starts making herself a coffee, and Ashildr hurries out of the pantry. I follow after him in a daze. It's not until we enter the elevator that Ashildr dips his head toward me and says in a low voice, "Not very competent, that one."

"Who, Ms. Ichor?"

He nods. "Rumor has it, Mr. Ferguson felt bad that he dumped her when they were kids, so he hired her out of pity."

Or he hired her to fuck with me. Why does that sound a lot more plausible?

"What *is* her job?" I ask.

"She's one of the discount-pricing coordinators," he says. "She handles the CLIFF initiative."

My eyebrow asks the obvious question.

"CLIFF stands for Customer Loyalty Integration For Future," Ashildr says. "The guy Tiffany replaced was named Cliff, so he contrived that project name, and it kind of stuck. The idea is, Mr. Ferguson is willing to have lower margins when opening our stores in up-and-coming neighborhoods, in the hope that we'll establish brand loyalty early on, and then, as the financial circumstances in the neighborhoods improve, the margins can do so as well."

How Machiavellian of Gunther. Except, if my neighborhood is anything to go by, he put the wrong person in charge of this particular project. The prices at our Munch & Crunch are high for everyone, not just for the fixed-income folks in my rent-controlled building.

The elevator stops and we exit into a gym, one that is to every other gym what a five-star hotel is to a hostel... of the type you get murdered in.

Besides fitness equipment, they have a hot tub, a steam room, a Finnish dry sauna, a pool, yoga classes, and massages by appointment. Ashildr doesn't say it, but I bet the amenities also include private sessions with a harem of male gigolos, a llama petting zoo, and a perk where once a month, each of the personal trainers will let you kick them in the privates.

"Is this subsidized, like the cafeteria?" I ask when we head for the elevator.

"No," Ashildr says. "It's free."

My mouth hangs open. "All free?" Picturing myself in all that luxury sounds too good to be true—not unlike all the free gingerbread the witch offered to Hansel and Gretel.

"Mr. Ferguson is invested in the health of his employees," Ashildr says proudly.

Yeah, sure. More like he did a cost-benefit analysis

which concluded that gym access will cut down on sick days and otherwise increase productivity.

"How long is our lunch?" I ask.

Ashildr presses an elevator button with the letter C on it, which must stand for cafeteria. "Mr. Ferguson believes in flexible hours. You can take an hour for lunch and an hour for the gym if you wish, as long as you're not otherwise involved with something time-sensitive, like a meeting. Just make sure you stay later to compensate for the extra hours."

Here, too, I bet there's some ruthless cost-benefit analysis at play. Something along the lines of "flexible hours improve employee loyalty and morale, and that boosts productivity." It might even have a CLIFF-like acronym. Maybe CLIT?

Before Ashildr can tell me more about the wonders of Munch & Crunch, the elevator opens and we tour the cafeteria—which is a misnomer. What this really should be called is a ritzy restaurant.

Hmm. The prices are pretty good, especially for lobster and caviar. Still, I have to be realistic. So long as there's free food in the pantry, I'll be sticking to that.

"Business lunches and dinners take place there," Ashildr explains, gesturing toward a separate room off to the side of the cafeteria, where I see a bunch of serious-looking people in suits. "And in that case, they're paid for by the company, of course."

"Noted," I say. "By the by, should we sit down and talk some business today?"

He grins. "I think Mr. Ferguson will monopolize your time."

And just like that, I've lost my appetite.

Ashildr's phone dings.

"Ah," he says after checking the message. "Your desk is ready."

We return to the executive floor. Not surprisingly, it's very posh, with offices upon offices, including the cushiest ones along the walls that have breathtaking views of the city.

In the biggest such office sits Gunther, his posture straight and his eyes lost in his computer screen.

"And that's yours," Ashildr says, gesturing to the office adjacent to Gunther's.

I tear my gaze away from my nemesis and check out the space. Damn. If I were a corporate ladder climber, I'd have an officegasm. The view from my office is out of this world, and there's enough space in there to dance a jig.

But there is a problem. Thanks to all the glass and the way my screen is facing, Gunther will be able to see what I'm looking at.

Oh, well. If I were him, I wouldn't trust me not to be on TikTok all day either.

"You like?" Ashildr asks.

I nod, speechless. Just how important is my new role?

"Your login password is set to your initials and the last four digits of your phone number. Some onboarding instructions are in your inbox." He gestures at an office nearby. "I'll be in there if you have any questions."

"Thanks." I enter my office, walk over to my monitor, and touch my keyboard.

Nothing happens.

I move the mouse.

Nope.

I look for a computer to turn on, without any success.

Hmm. I turn the monitor on and off.

That doesn't help.

I guess I already have a question—and possibly a dumb one at that.

Exiting my office, I step into Ashildr's—and nearly bump into a contraption with water.

"Sorry," Ashildr says. "That's my air humidifier."

Is that why his office feels a little like a sauna?

"I need it," Ashildr explains. "Or else I get nosebleeds."

I stop in my tracks and try to hold in the sudden burst of terror.

Ashildr frowns. "Are you okay?"

How can I explain when I'm not even sure myself why this bothers me so much? All I know is, my blood aversion has grown worse in recent years, and I've just learned that he could've bled from his face at any point during our acquaintance. I shudder. That is as close to my worst nightmare as it gets. The only thing scarier is visiting one of those labs where they do blood draws.

I have no clue what my cholesterol is, and I will probably never find out.

"I'm fine," I somehow manage to say, albeit not very convincingly. "I wanted to ask... How do I turn on my computer?" And where is it?

He smacks himself on the forehead. "Our computers are built into the monitor." He points at a little hole near his monitor's camera. "That's a microphone. To turn the system on, you use a voice command." He moves his face closer to the mic and says, "Octothorpe, I'm done Munching and Crunching."

"Shutting down," a chipmunk-y voice says from the monitor speakers. The computer shuts down, and the monitor goes black.

I grin. "Octothorpe?" It sounds like a werewolf with eight heads and would be a great safeword for a BDSM couple who are very into Scrabble.

Ashildr brings his face to the mic again. "Octothorpe, let's Munch and Crunch."

"Starting up," the chipmunk says.

The monitor turns back on, and a login screen shows up.

"I bet you can tell that the word is designed to get the attention of our AI assistant," he says. "It's actually another term for the hashtag symbol. Mr. Fonzov—the creator of this product—thinks that a synonym for a hashtag makes a better command word than something like Siri or Alexa."

"And this command word will make everything you

tell your computer sound like a bunch of social media hashtags."

"You're right," Ashildr says as I start to leave. "Now, hashtag werkwerkwerk."

Smiling, I dash for my office.

Once there, I tentatively say, "Octothorpe."

I'm about to continue, but I must be too slow because the chipmunk voice pipes up. "I await your command."

My command? I knew BDSM was afoot.

"Let's Munch and Crunch," I say in my best mistress impersonation, even though I feel pretty goofy.

"Starting up," the chipmunk says obediently, and my machine lights up.

I use the info provided to log in and change the password when prompted to "GuntherIsAnAs$h01e."

First, I check the intro email and begin the onboarding activities as advised. It's all so boring I feel like I should've asked Gunther for more money—or accepted jailtime.

Hopefully, this is a one-time pain.

Deciding to liven things up, I take out my phone, curse myself for forgetting my headphones, and set *Spiderman* by the Ramones to play as loudly as the tiny phone speakers allow.

There. Better. I resume the tedious activity.

When I get to HR policies, one stands out:

"If you start dating a coworker, please fill out HR form 66669."

Hmm. So… dating someone you work with is allowed

here? What if one of you owns the company? Surely, that's an iffy power dynamic. Not that I'm at any risk of being in that situation. I hate Gunther too much for that, and he hates me. I'm more worried about Tiffany, in case he hired her out of amorous intent rather than pity.

Yeah. That's it. I'm concerned solely about Tiffany.

And sidebar—form 66669? That combines the number of the beast *and* a sexual position—not exactly something that makes you want to trust said form.

Oh, well. I locate PowerPoint on my desktop and do my best to prepare myself for the inevitable conversation with Gunther. I must lose myself in that task because I'm startled when someone knocks on my office door.

I pivot in my chair.

It's Gunther, and he looks dashing, damn him.

"Come in," I say, and then, unsure of the protocol, I stand up.

As soon as he's in, he winces. "What is that horrible noise?"

I glare at him. "You mean the best song of all time?"

"Turn it off before my ears bleed."

The horrid image makes my skin break into gooseflesh, but I do my best not to show any weakness in front of my adversary and simply turn the music off.

Gunther looks me over from head to foot. "Do you think that's a suitable outfit for today?"

I look down. I'm wearing my usual leather jacket, a Sex Pistols T-shirt, bondage pants, and platform leather boots—an outfit not very different from what I had on when he last saw me and blackmailed me into this job. "What's wrong with my clothes?"

If a sigh could have shoulders, the one that escapes his mouth would carry the weight of the world. "Munch & Crunch isn't a biker gang."

A chuckle escapes my lips.

He scowls at me.

"Munch & Crunch sounds like the lamest biker gang name possible," I say. "Unless they're cannibals."

His scowl doesn't show any chinks. "We have a business casual dress code in this building. I expect you to follow it."

I scoff. "I don't have money for new outfits. If you care about that shit, you buy it."

"Language," he growls.

"Ex-fucking-cuse me?"

"I expect you to refrain from using obscenities in my building."

"Do I need to perform an exorcism?" I ask.

Huh. I've finally wiped that self-assured look from his smug face.

"What are you talking about?" he demands.

"You sound possessed—by a ghost of a governess with a broom up her ass."

His only reply is something unintelligible under his breath.

"Language," I chide, doing my best to sound like him.

His nostrils flare. "I didn't... never mind. Can we finally talk coupons?"

"The word 'finally' implies it's *me* who's been wasting our time on tangents about what's proper for a lady to wear and say."

"Right, a lady." He turns his back to me. "See you in Meeting Room A."

With that, he strides away—and since he's not headed to his office, I assume it's to the meeting room in question. I follow, but his legs are longer, so I have trouble keeping up. At some point when he turns the corner, I lose sight of him.

Great. Where the fuck is that meeting room?

Spotting a bathroom, I use it, then retrace my steps and ask Ashildr where to go.

When I get to my destination, Gunther, Tiffany, and a few people I haven't met are sitting there, looking impatient.

"Ms. Hyman," Gunther says coldly. "Thanks for making the time." He then proceeds to introduce everyone in the room, including 'Ms. Ichor'—like he doesn't know that I know her, as intimately as only a stabber can know her stabbee.

I battle a rare-for-me spurt of shyness as all eyes stay on me. "How do I get something on the TV screen?" I ask, pushing past the uncomfortable sensation. "I prepared a little presentation."

Gunther looks flabbergasted, like I've just told him I built a ballistic missile all by myself. Nonetheless, he grabs the laptop next to him, does something so that his screen shows up on the TV, then logs out and gestures for me to log in to my account. When I do that, my presentation is there on the desktop—indicating that the file lives somewhere in the Munch & Crunch corporate cloud.

"Thanks." I pull up my first slide. "To start, I figured I'd go over the features of coupons that someone who likes to abuse them loves—be that a regular couponer or someone more nefarious." I proceed to explain all the features, feeling like a traitor as I go.

Everyone except Tiffany looks impressed, and a few people are actually even taking notes.

I go to my next slide. "Now on to more shady business." I tell them about some techniques a hypothetical evil genius might use to create a fraudulent coupon, like changing the percent-off number on a real coupon—say, making ten percent into seventy. I then go into more dastardly scenarios, like manufacturing a coupon from scratch using a special printer and special paper.

Again, everyone gives me their rapt attention, even Tiffany.

Feeling a boost of confidence, I switch slides. "Before I talk about possible countermeasures, I have a question. Does Munch & Crunch have control over coupons that go into magazines, newspapers, and coupon books?"

A stern woman whose last name I've already forgotten shakes her head. "Not the paper and ink. We just give them the digital creative."

"Makes sense," I say and switch slides. "In that case, here are some solutions." I tell them a few ideas I've come up with—like making sure there's always a barcode to scan on the coupon, even if their store doesn't plan to scan. "It takes balls to forge a coupon with a scannable code," I say. "And even bigger ones to waltz into the store and use it."

Gunther's expression is hard to read. He's either itching to chastise me for saying 'balls' or is on the verge of applauding my brilliance.

I share my other ideas, including what I dislike as an old-school coupon junky—digital coupons.

"Any questions?" I say when I get to the end of my PowerPoint.

"What's the budget for this?" the stern woman asks… sternly.

The number Gunther gives shocks me, but everyone looks nonchalant.

"Have you decided who will lead this effort?" Tiffany asks, and it's clear she desperately wants to volunteer herself—for this project, as well as for Gunther's bed.

"I thought that would be obvious," Gunther says. "Her."

Everyone gapes at where his finger is pointing.

My heart skips a beat, and I suddenly feel like I've been surrounded by the aforementioned cannibalistic bikers.

Gunther is pointing at me.

Six

"But she's new," the stern woman says.

Tiffany nods at her approvingly. "She's also barely—"

"Are my decisions ever up for debate?" Gunther interrupts, eyes narrowing.

"No, sir," everyone mutters.

He stands up. "In that case, this meeting is adjourned."

Everyone leaves, but I sit there, still stunned.

"How am I supposed to lead a project?" I ask no one in particular.

"With my help, of course," Gunther says, startling me. I didn't even notice he'd stayed behind.

"Oh?"

"How about I give you a crash course?" he says.

"Do I have a choice?"

"No," he says, and then does exactly as he suggested —delivers a course so boring that it crashes my brain a few times along the way. I learn things like what a project management life cycle is, and how it goes at Munch & Crunch. Between the lines, I also learn how much Gunther likes his acronyms and corporate jargon. My favorite from today is probably the SoW, which stands for Statement of Work, though for me, it brings to mind Petunia the pig, a sow on my parents' farm. Mom likes to tell the story of how she brought said sow to orgasm as part of artificial insemination.

Yeah. I have a theory that having so many daughters might've caused something in Mom's mind to snap (possibly Dad's too). There are eight of us in total— before my clutch, they'd had twins. Not that such excuses made Petunia feel any better about the violation of her person.

"So," Gunther says, bringing me out of swine-related thoughts. "How about you work on the SoW?"

"Do I have a choice?" I ask again. Because I'd rather repeat my mom's dubious achievement with Petunia.

He shakes his head. "This is your only way out of a mess that you yourself created."

"I guess I'll work on the damn pig... I mean SoW."

His dark eyebrows pull together dangerously. "Have I just wasted my time?"

"You ever get tired of being Mr. Dictator? I said I'll work on the stupid thing, and I will."

He gestures at the laptop. "You can take that in case you need to work remotely or during your commute. If you need any supplies, talk to Ashildr. He's the executive assistant."

The deal-loving part of me is unreasonably thrilled about a free laptop—even if the rational part of me knows that this is the same kind of "free" as in the proverbial free lunch. For instance, if I decide to play hooky by pretending to be sick, this laptop will be an impediment.

"Can Ashildr arrange for a chip in my brain—to make sure I can work when I'm in the shower?" I ask.

Gunther stands up. "If you don't want the laptop, you don't have to take it."

With that, he leaves.

I check the sleek gizmo. The last time I saw one like it on sale, it was a thousand dollars, and I couldn't afford it. In other words, of course I'll take it. In fact, the next thing I do is swing by Ashildr's office to find out where I can get a laptop carrying case—because I can't not protect my shiny new toy from scratches.

"Let me show you the supply room," Ashildr says and leads me to what turns out to be the promised land.

Staples, Post-it notes, notebooks, calendars, desk organizers, and all wonderfully free!

"Before you ask, if you need to take anything home, you can," Ashildr says.

"Is there a shopping cart I can borrow?" I whisper in awe.

He chuckles nervously. "No. Only what you can carry."

Challenge accepted. With Ashildr's help, I carry

enough stuff to my office to run an Office Depot, and maybe a Staples, for a week.

"I'll let you get settled," Ashildr says and escapes before I can use him as my mule again.

I set up my office with all the freebies, then start the stupid SoW.

When I get hungry, I head over to the pantry to case out the snacks. Wow. Somebody brought in even more food. For once, however, I don't dive right for it because something odd catches my eye.

A big jar with a thick yellowish liquid and a note:

Honey—for everyone's pleasure.

Grinding my teeth, I fight the urge to smash the jar against the wall. I know that handwriting. I saw it on all the documents I recently signed. Gunther wrote that—and left the honey, all as part of some asinine prank.

Is this some sort of hazing? But the choice of words… "Pleasure?" "Everyone?" Is he saying I'm the office slut? Also, the honey jar joke is so incredibly unoriginal. If I had a quarter for every time someone somehow linked my name to the bees' bodily fluids, I'd be able to swim in money by now, like Scrooge McDuck.

I march into Gunther's office to tell him exactly what I think, but find him missing.

Hmm. Maybe this is an opportunity.

I sprint to the supply room and grab all the pink Post-it notes that I can carry, then return to Gunther's office. With an evil grin, I start sticking the notes in the pattern I have in mind—including on the windows, on the monitor, on the keyboard, on the floor, and on his chair.

When I'm done, I look it over and laugh.

The office was cold and modern before, but with all that pink, it looks like Barbie's Dreamhouse.

Grinning, I return to my office and install a rearview mirror on my monitor—so I can see Gunther's reaction when he comes back to see my handiwork.

After waiting a couple of minutes, I realize I've forgotten to eat, so I take care of that.

Gunther still isn't back.

Oh, well. For now, I can work on the SoW to kill the time.

"Octothorpe, let's Munch and Crunch," I say giddily.

"Starting up," the chipmunk voice says, sounding more cheerful than earlier—obscenely so. Maybe the computer mimes my emotions?

I get to work, but really, I'm waiting.

And waiting.

And waiting some more. Gunther doesn't come back after an hour. Or two hours. Or three.

Even after I finish the document, he still hasn't shown up.

Bastard. He deserves some kind of award for managing to annoy me by *not* being around.

My stomach rumbles, so I visit the luxurious pantry once more.

The jar of honey is there, with some of its contents missing.

Oh, no. People are actually helping themselves to the honey? Fuck that. I grab a couple of protein bars and some fruit in one hand, and the offending jar in the other.

"This thing is going home with me," I say, in case I'm being recorded by a surveillance camera. "I will not be humiliated a second longer."

Stomping back to my office, I eat at my desk and stare at the clock.

Way past five.

He's probably not coming back.

Fine.

I snatch the jar from my desk and head home.

———

There are packages waiting for me by the door.

Odd. I didn't order anything.

I take them inside and open them one by one.

What the fuck? It's clothes and shoes.

It can't be… can it?

Yup. There's a note from Gunther:

Office-appropriate attire. After your first paycheck, I expect you to purchase more on your own.

Huh. There are seven outfits here. Why would I ever waste money on more?

Lethally soft footsteps catch my attention. I turn to see Bunny's evil eyes gleaming with curiosity.

It-that-feeds-me will let me play with those boxes—or it will end up skinned inside a box... and in the ground.

"All yours," I tell him, getting all the stuff out.

Bunny promptly paws at the shoebox, as if it were something small, furry, and cute.

I leave the honey jar in the kitchen and start trying everything on.

I look like a fucking librarian, but it all fits, even the shoes.

Did one of my sisters help Gunther with this? Prior to today, having one of them try shit on for me was the only way not to shop in person.

I sigh.

I guess I'll have to play dress-up tomorrow.

Seven

To my huge disappointment, the Post-its are all gone as I walk past Gunther's office the next morning.

No, not gone.

Gunther is holding a big wad of them as he intercepts me on my way to my office. "Is this what you did yesterday instead of working on the SoW?"

"Good morning, *Gunther*." The day I call him Mr. Ferguson is the day I'll need my spleen examined. "Nice to see you. How are things?"

"I should've known," he growls. "You said you'd—"

"Shut it," I snap. "I finished the fucking SoW. Want to see?"

He looks startled—though I'm not sure if it's because of my f-bomb or the fact that I did an honest day's work.

"Come." I lead him to my desk, get Octothorpe to open my workstation, and display the fruits of my labor on the screen—all without sitting down.

"Great job," he says after examining it, sounding annoyingly surprised.

I feel a stupid, unwelcome burst of pride. I do my best to suppress it. "Next time, get the facts first. So far, I've done everything you've asked, even donned this hideous outfit."

He looks me up and down, his emerald eyes gleaming with something—probably anger.

"You think you look professional?" he finally asks, sounding incredulous.

I look down. "I have a blouse and a skirt on."

He points at my right forearm. "Is that a tattoo of Snow White with a shotgun, wearing a Guy Fawkes mask?"

"This is not the 1950s," I say with an eyeroll. "It's not just criminals who get tattoos nowadays."

He points at my left forearm. "Is that a demon sodomizing a mime?"

I shrug. "You sent me clothes, I put them on."

He gives me a hard look. "Expect another batch— this time with long sleeves."

"Fine. Whatever." I gesture at the door. "Don't you have somewhere to be?"

His eyes narrow further. "I need to tell you what to work on next." He nods at my chair. "Have a seat."

I plop into my chair—and nearly have a heart attack.

At first, it sounds like a dozen cats are having sex in my ears, but then I realize what it really is.

A bullhorn.

When I catch my breath, I check my theory.

Yep.

Someone duct-taped a bullhorn under my chair.

Based on the fingers in Gunther's ears and the smug expression on his face, I don't have to guess who the culprit is.

"I have a younger brother," Gunther says, smirking. "When it comes to pranks, you're in over your head."

I snort. "Did you forget that I have seven sisters? You know Gia, right?"

He looks less self-assured, and for good reason. My older sister, Gia, grew up to be a magician—as in a professional trickster. When she was young, her sadistic creativity when it came to pranks was the stuff of legend.

Swiftly composing himself, he gestures imperiously at the screen. "Let's talk about the three Ps of project planning," he says and proceeds to talk for a while, telling me things so boring no mortal ears should be subjected to them. Eventually, he gets around to assigning me a related task and leaves.

I detach the bullhorn from under my chair and plan out my next attack before starting on my assignment.

At 9:30, Gunther leaves his desk.

This is my chance. I grab a piece of duct tape and sprint to his office. Turning over his mouse, I tape over the laser sensor and run back.

By the time I'm in my chair, I see him come back.

He grabs the mouse.

Wiggles it.

His face looks annoyed.

He wiggles it again.

I crack up.

He messes with the thing for another minute, then turns it over.

Once he spots the duct tape, he throws a death-ray stare at my office. I wait for him to come over and yell at me, but he doesn't. He just rips off the tape and gets to working on whatever it is CEOs do.

And looks sexy doing it, the bastard.

Ugh. Well, at least I got him good.

For the next two hours, my productivity is boosted by gloating. It's not until I feel hunger pangs that I realize leaving my office will open me up for retaliation.

Oh, well.

I head to the pantry and grab a bunch of snacks. On the cappuccino machine, I notice a new sign: *Now voice-activated*.

Huh. I grab a cup and put it under the dispenser. "Octothorpe. Make coffee."

Nothing happens.

"Octothorpe. Cappuccino time."

Nada.

After attempt number six, I hear a snort.

It's Gunther, leaning against the doorway with a gleeful smirk on his face. "I can't believe you fell for that."

Without meaning to, I advance on him, not sure if the plan is to smack or lick that smirk off his face.

"You're going to regret starting this feud," I say when I'm so far into his personal space I can smell him—something alluringly masculine with notes of burned candles, which brings to mind a romantically adorned bedroom.

His smirk is gone—score for me. "*I* started it?"

Like a moth attracted to a candle's flame, I sway closer to him. I'm having trouble thinking for some reason, but I still manage to say, "You're the one who left that jar with a suggestion to use me for pleasure."

His features darken. "I leave honey here on a weekly basis."

My mouth suddenly feels dry, so I moisten my lips. "Why?"

He looks hungry—probably needs his lunch. "In my spare time, I'm a beekeeper."

I blink up at him. "Bees? Where did you find bees?" I've always pictured him living in a Manhattan penthouse—but never with a beehive inside, or even on the roof.

"My bees live next to my house," he says. "In New Jersey."

Oh. He lives in Jersey. I didn't know that. There's a lot more space there—too much even.

"For real?" I ask.

It would explain that subtle scent that is pleasantly tickling my nose. It's not candles. It's beeswax and smoke.

He leans down so our eyes are level. "As much as

you feel that the world revolves around you, that's not the case."

Fuck. If I wanted to kiss him, my lips would only need to traverse a few measly inches. "How was I supposed to know you're a beekeeper?"

He straightens, waving my question off. "The only thing you were supposed to know is that I'd never write such a vile thing."

This time, I'm not sure why I moisten my lips. "About me specifically or your employees in general?"

His eyes flash green. "If you're going to manage projects, you need to learn to be a better judge of character."

A swarm of bees mutinies in my belly—no doubt demanding that Gunther use his particular set of skills to tame them. "I *am* a great judge of character."

Gunther lowers his head toward me again. "The evidence is to the contrary."

What can I retort? I can't very well claim that my common sense failed me because of *him*. Or that it's failing me now. How else do I explain drawing closer to him, as if I were pulled by bees holding invisible strings? My heartbeat accelerates, my breath turning shallow as an uncomfortable warmth gathers deep inside me, making me acutely aware of my body and the unfamiliar clothes confining it—and the way his soft-looking lips part as he stares down at me with dawning comprehension. The way his eyes turn a brighter emerald as he dips his head toward me and—

Someone clears his throat, uncomfortably.

I jerk away from Gunther.

Ashildr—the throat clearer—looks like he wants to be anywhere but here, including inside a beehive.

"So… beekeeping," I say breathlessly to Gunther. "Why not? It's a good deal. The bees get an opportunity to sting you, and you get free honey in return."

If I had a chance to bite him, I'd also give up some of my bodily fluids, I'm sure.

Gunther's expression is difficult to puzzle out as he steps back and also clears his throat. "Yeah, it's relaxing to be with them." He readjusts his tie, looking at me. "What about you? Any hobbies?"

Doing a poor job of pretending that this conversation is normal, Ashildr walks over to the coffee machine and begins to brew something. To my chagrin, he doesn't fall for the "voice activated" bit.

I return my attention to Gunther and do my best to continue the pretense. "You know I like sales and deals."

"That's not a hobby," Gunther replies, apparently getting into the spirit of things.

I scoff. "It is too. How is collecting coupons different from collecting stamps? Besides, I also own a metal detector and use it on the beach. That's a hobby, for sure."

He shrugs. "Fine. That one qualifies, maybe."

I perk up. "I also forage for mushrooms. Which isn't all that different from beekeeping, though way safer."

Gunther snorts. "Mushrooms could be poisonous."

"Not if you take your mycologist friend with you when you go pick them."

Ashildr scurries out of the pantry like a mouse being chased by Bunny.

An awkward silence falls between us. Clearly, the hobbies conversation has run its course. So what now? Did I imagine what happened—or almost happened—earlier? A part of me wants to go near him again, but a much saner part tells that other part to get a fucking clue.

"I'd better go," Gunther says, throwing cold water on all of my parts. "I've got an appointment."

"Sure," I say dubiously.

He frowns. "I really do. My iron is high, so I donate blood at the beginning of every month."

Why would he say *that*, of all things? My skin instantly grows clammy, and I feel faint.

Of all human activity, nothing scares me more than a blood draw. I'm more scared of that medical procedure than my sister Blue is of rabid birds. I don't know why this is, but the mere thought of it can send me into a nauseating spiral. Same goes for the sight of a leech. Or an overfed mosquito.

"Are you okay?" Gunther asks, his voice sounding oddly distant, as if I'm hearing it through a tunnel. "I'm sorry if you thought I was about to do something inappropriate earlier. I would never."

Wait, what? I snap back to full attention. So I didn't imagine the almost-kiss? I forget all about the procedure that shall not be mentioned and stare at Gunther, mouth agape.

He stares back at me, looking worried. As he should be. I mean, why commit so strongly to no kissing? As Charles Dickens famously said, "Never say never."

"It's not that," I manage to squeeze out. "I think my sugar is low."

"Oh." He does his signature eye narrowing bit. "In that case, eat something. That's an order."

I snort. "This isn't the army. You can't order me around."

"You're on my payroll. If I ask you to eat on company time, you'll eat." He sounds like a drill sergeant.

Wait, why am I thinking about drilling? Specifically, hard drilling? I blink and try to gather my wayward thoughts. "Okay, I'll eat. Go do your thing." And please don't repeat what it is.

He nods imperiously. "Good. I want to see you bite something. Now."

Gulp. Why does that make me think of biting... things? Inappropriate things? Like succulent lips and— "Okay," I squeak and grab the first thing I spot on the counter—a nut bar.

Under his determined stare, I rip open the wrapper and bite. Hard.

"Good girl," he murmurs, eyes half-lidded. Then, apparently realizing how that came out, he clears his throat and says, "That is, good job."

Turning, he leaves so fast I can't help but think he's escaping.

I stare after him, chewing mindlessly. I can't believe what has just happened. Or almost happened? I'm not sure. I also can't believe he wasn't the one to start our prank war. Still, he got me good, and the ball is in my court. I refuse to let him have the last word. My reputation as a person with seven sisters is at stake.

So, after I recover from what may or may not have happened, I gather my munchies, drop them on my desk, and visit Gunther's office, where I swap his Bluetooth keyboard for mine.

Grinning in anticipation, I switch to working on my laptop and wait for him to return.

———

"Did you eat more?" I hear Gunther ask, out of nowhere.

I swallow my heart back into my chest and swivel my chair to face him—all six-feet-plus of him. "You startled me."

How did I not see him come into my office? I must've gotten caught up in work, boring though it may be.

"Sorry," he says, sounding not the least bit apologetic. "Now answer the question."

I roll my eyes. "Yes, mother. My tummy is full. Now go." I make shooing motions. "Let me work."

He closes the office door, and I watch him in the rearview mirror I installed.

As he sits at his desk, I Google the lyrics to *Gangnam Style*.

When I see Gunther beginning to type, I copy-paste said lyrics and enjoy the confused expression on his face as he reads lines and lines of K-Pop suddenly appearing in the middle of some important email he was drafting. Unless he speaks Korean, the only discernible words in that song are "Eh, sexy lady" and "style."

Annoyingly quickly, Gunther leaps to his feet, grabs the keyboard, storms into my office, and swaps the keyboards without saying a word.

Sore loser much?

Oh, well.

I resume my work. All is well for a while, but then my phone rings—a landline I didn't realize I had.

Warily, I pick up.

"Hello," says an elderly lady's voice.

"Hi," I say. "How can I help you?"

"Ashildr, is that you, sweetie?" the lady asks. "You have to speak up. My hearing aid broke."

"This isn't Ashildr," I say louder. "Who is this? I can tell him you called."

"You caught a cold?" she asks.

"No," I shout. "I'm not Ashildr."

"What did you call me?"

"I didn't call you anything. I was just saying I'm not—"

In the distance, I hear laughter, so I belatedly look in the mirror.

Fuck.

Gunther is holding his phone and looking right at me. "I told you, I have a younger brother." The sentence coming out of my phone starts out sounding like the old lady but morphs into Gunther's voice halfway.

Grunting in frustration, I slam down the phone—a pleasure that isn't possible with smartphones.

For the next several hours, I don't bother with pranks. I feel like I'm losing, so I have to get him good. And as a bonus, thinking about pranks keeps me from thinking about other things. Like what Gunther admitted. And what I refuse to admit.

Around four p.m., the stern lady that I met yesterday knocks on my office door.

"Enter," I say reluctantly.

What does she want?

She strides in, her expression unreadable. "I'm Ms. Severina," she states. "We met at the coupon improvement kick-off meeting."

"Sure," I say. "Good to see you again." I want to ask what the fuck she's doing here, but I worry she'll chastise me for language even more than Gunther has.

"Mr. Ferguson requested that I walk you through our current coupon creation process," she says. "If it's not a good time…"

"No." I close the file I was almost done with anyway. "I've been curious about said process."

She looks around with disapproval. "Why don't you have a guest chair?"

She must be the life of every party. "I'll get you one."

I head over to a nearby empty office and grab the least comfortable of the chairs I see there. Rolling it into my office, I gesture for her to sit.

"Can I drive?" she asks.

I move away from my keyboard. "Mi casa es su casa."

She takes over and shows me the ropes—and beats Gunther in every single way when it comes to making the subject matter boring.

Still, there's a light at the end of this tunnel. An idea for an epic prank begins to brew in my mind, one so devious my sister Gia would be proud.

At around five, Ms. Severina pauses the lesson. "If you're one of those nine-to-five people, we can resume tomorrow." She makes working from nine to five sound worse than torture, cannibalism, and price-gouging combined.

"I'm okay to continue," I say. Given the flexible hours at this place, I can always take a longer lunch or check out the gym tomorrow to compensate.

Nodding approvingly, Severina keeps droning on, and I listen, suppressing a yawn throughout. As the clock ticks on, I can't help but notice that Gunther is still in his office.

"When does he leave?" I ask Severina when she asks if I have any questions.

For the first time, her stern expression shows a crack. "Mr. Ferguson is always the last to leave."

"Oh? Poor guy. We're keeping him away from his bees."

She almost smiles at that. "We carry his honey at some of our stores," she whispers proudly. "The brand is Buzz Beerin."

I grin. "Doesn't that sound more like a name for a beer?"

Her stern expression is back. "It's a very clever name for honey. Buzz is the sound the bees make, and then there's Buzz Aldrin, a famous astronaut who—"

"Oh, I get it." The best jokes are always the ones you have to explain ad nauseam.

Then it hits me. Buzz Beerin could be part of my prank idea. It's perfect for that.

I go for it. "Has there ever been a sale on Buzz Beerin?" I ask, doing my best to sound nonchalant.

She shakes her head. "Not yet."

Almost there. "It would be nice to create some coupons, to really understand the system," I say. "Buzz Beerin sounds like a good product to practice on."

Her eyes gleam. "Perhaps one of our digital discounts."

Score! "Yeah. Sure. If you think that's best."

Her thin fingers fly over the keyboard excitedly, and soon, there's a coupon for Buzz Beerin—ten percent off sticker price, to be exact.

"This is how you set the promotion date." She hovers the mouse cursor over the icon on the right.

"I'm going to set it to a few weeks from today. That should give the merchandising team and everyone else enough time."

"Great." I rub my eyes. "Now if you don't mind, I think I'd like to head home for the day. I'm starving and tired."

"I was actually almost done," she says and clicks the email button on the form in front of us. "I'll put your email down so you'll be notified when this goes live." She then clicks the "save" button—which is right next to "undo."

"Thanks so much," I say pointedly.

She stands up reluctantly. "Let me know if you have any more questions."

"Will do."

I wait until she leaves, and then I check my rearview mirror to make sure Gunther hasn't snuck over to look over my shoulder.

Nope. I'm safe.

Feeling extremely naughty, I change the ten percent off to one hundred and ten—meaning a customer would actually get paid if they purchased Buzz Beerin as part of this promo.

As I bring the cursor over to click "save," I hesitate.

Given that Gunther brought me here to Honey-proof his coupon operation, would he think this prank crosses the line? Or worse, see it not as a prank but as me getting back to my shenanigans?

Crap. I hate it when I grow a conscience all of a sudden. I click "undo" and close the file before I get tempted again. I'll have to come up with some other prank—something that isn't coupon-related.

Feeling surprisingly proud of my restraint, I get up to leave.

Gunther stays put.

I pop my head into his office. "Good night."

"See you tomorrow," he says, his eyes not leaving the screen. "Don't forget to eat."

Eight

HAVING EATEN, AS I WAS ORDERED, I DEAL WITH THE
packages I found when I got home.

As I suspected, it's clothes—proper attire, long-
sleeve edition.

Bunny looks at me skeptically when I try one
outfit on.

*It-that-feeds-me's survival chances just went down. It
now looks too much like other members of its litter—and it
should know how fervently I desire to make catnip toys out
of their skins.*

———

The next morning, Gunther isn't in his office, so I pop
in and set up my next prank, using rubber bands and
duct tape to rig an air freshener bottle to spray
continuously.

When it starts to hiss, I run.

Damn.

In the time it takes me to escape, the scent is already so strong that my smell-sensitive sister Lemon would probably die on the spot. I can't even imagine how bad it will be when the bottle is emptied.

Maybe I overdid it?

Too late now.

When I get to my office, I frown.

The smell from Gunther's office is seeping into mine.

Damn. It smells like a perfume factory blew up in here. How bad is it at the epicenter? Whatever. The expression on Gunther's face will make this nuisance worth it.

Hopefully.

I sit behind my desk and blink at my screen.

"You've got a virus," the screen states.

How? This is a corporate computer. Shouldn't it have an anti-virus program or something? I should call the IT department... except that phone number is stored in Outlook, as in, computer required for access.

The good news is my laptop is with me, so I log in there and pull up the number I need—which is when I spot Gunther walking into his office.

IT can wait.

I watch his expression.

Fucker. Acting as if nothing at all is the matter, Gunther walks up to his window and opens it.

These things actually open?

I sprint to mine.

Nope. No sign of a latch or anything. Which makes sense. Windows and the corporate world do not mix. After hearing a lecture about project management, too many people would give in to the temptation to jump.

Someone knocks on my office door.

It's Gunther.

"Come in," I say grudgingly.

He walks in and theatrically wrinkles his nose. "I know HR didn't explicitly say so, but too much perfume is frowned upon."

"Why don't I have a window that opens?" I demand.

He shrugs. "Liability?"

"But yours does."

His full lips turn up in that annoying smirk. "There are perks to being in charge."

I take a step toward him. "About yesterday..."

He frowns. "I'm not sure what you're talking about."

I sigh. "What happened in the pantry..." The almost-kiss I had X-rated dreams about.

He feigns a look of confusion. "You mean my awesome coffee-machine prank? Or the hobbies discussion?"

So that's how he wants to play it—pretend nothing happened? It's probably for the best, but it pisses me off for some reason.

"Beekeeping is a job, not a hobby," I say snidely. "And that prank was just so-so. Mine would be much better if you didn't have a window."

He grins devilishly. "So... you still think seven sisters beats a younger brother?" Before I can answer, he walks over to my screen and, to my shock, removes a laminated paper that was covering it.

A paper with "You've got a virus" printed on it.

Damn. That's almost a Gia-level trick. Not that I'd ever tell him that. "I still say seven sisters will triumph. If nothing else, I could have five of them come over and make you think you're seeing me everywhere."

He checks out my long-sleeved getup. "It might almost work." He scans my face. "Assuming they'd all be willing to pierce their noses and eyebrows, that is."

"Don't forget tongues," I say and stick mine out to display the stud I have in it.

Is that horror or something else in his gaze? It's gone too quickly, replaced by a theatrical eyeroll. "Would your sisters also stick their tongues out at me, like five-year-olds?"

I hate him more when he makes good points. It's just as well I didn't catalogue my other piercings that he can't see—like in my nipples, my belly button, and my most private area that I've codenamed Pot.

"So," he says, his tone turning serious in a flash. "How about we talk about your next task in my office, where the air is fresher?"

———

The next day, I sneak into Gunther's office and replace the pictures of his family with those of Ted Bundy, John Wayne Gacy, and Ronald McDonald.

His retaliation is swift and evil. When I bite into a

yummy-looking caramel apple that I find in the pantry, it turns out to be an onion. Apparently, Gunther made the "treat" and warned the rest of the floor to keep away from it.

I consult Gia for my next day's move, and Gunther finds a realistic-looking group of creepy crawlies in his desk drawer.

The following day, I find my office filled to the brim with balloons. I nearly deafen myself popping them, then speak in a high-pitched tone from all the helium I end up inhaling.

We prank each other back and forth for the rest of the week. On Monday, when Gunther catches me planting a glitter bomb, he sternly states, "This needs to stop."

I look at him innocently. "What?"

"My productivity is down," he says. "Yours too, I imagine."

I stand straighter. "I've done all my work. On time." Then again, I'd probably be able to take on extra work if I didn't waste so much time thinking up pranks. Or better yet, I'd leave early.

He sighs. "Fine. We stop for *my* sake."

I grin diabolically. "As in, you're giving up?"

"Is that what it would take?"

"It would be a start. Also, I could use another source of entertainment."

His dark eyebrows pull together. "You're here to work."

I act as though I'm about to drop my glitter bomb. "If that's how you want to play it, I'm not sure if—"

"How about coupons?" he asks in an exasperated voice.

I clap my eyelashes at him. "What coupons?"

"Before hiring you, we had a bunch of competitor coupons stockpiled for research. Would it be entertaining for you to check them out?"

Would a bear like access to the fruit of Gunther's bees' labor? "Yes, please," I exclaim, only to realize I've been had.

Coupons are work-related, after all, and the gleam in his eyes shows that he knows that.

"Great." He gestures at the door to his office. "I'll make sure you get that tour by the end of today."

"Deal." I turn to head out, then stop. "Oh, and I accept your defeat."

————

Someone knocks on my office door after lunch. Turning, I see Tiffany, who looks like she's swallowed some shit-laced lemons.

"Mr. Ferguson asked me to give you a tour of the coupon repository," she says after I reluctantly wave her in. "Is now a good time?"

He asked *her* to do something with *me*? Is the prank war back on, or is this more sinister? I did suspect he got me here as revenge for my sins of the past, and having Tiffany be part of said revenge would be poetic justice.

"Now works." I should win an award for how cordial I keep my tone. "Lead the way."

With a bitchy huff, Tiffany leads me to the elevator, and we take a silent ride to the basement, the air between us crackling with attitude the whole time.

"This way," she says and leads me down a corridor.

Hmm. A place without witnesses. Is she going to eat my liver?

Maybe. For the moment, she points to the card reader next to a plain-looking door. "Try it. You should have access."

I wave my card over it, and the lock clicks open. She holds the door for me as I enter.

Holy Black Friday! It's like I've arrived on my home planet.

There's a million dollars' worth of coupons in here —and that's a conservative estimate.

Tiffany must read my expression. "Before you decide to take any home, you should know that they've been fully catalogued."

"Are you calling me a thief?" The urge to take out my knife is strong, but I fight it, this being a place of work and all that. Not to mention, this idiot could stab herself again, and her blood is the last thing I want to see.

"If the shoe fits." She drops her gaze to my work-appropriate pumps. "Unlike those."

I take a step toward her. "What did you say?"

She backs away. "You're not Munch & Crunch material, and you know it."

I cock my head. "And *you* are?"

"He hired you out of pity," she says. "Obviously."

I wave my hand like a beauty pageant winner. "I'm going to call you Pot from now on. You can call me Kettle." Pot is currently my vagina's nickname, but they can share it.

Tiffany spins around. "Find your own way back."

As she stomps off, I call out, "You mean walk down a corridor?"

No reply.

Fine. Whatever. Hopefully, the next time Gunther asks her to do something that involves me, she'll refuse.

———

Without pranks, the next couple of weeks are humdrum, and the only positive thing I can say about my work is that I turn out to be good at it, and not just the coupon-related parts.

What sucks is that Gunther continues to be purely professional, only talking about work and nothing else. Needless to say, he keeps pretending the thing in the pantry never happened. As time passes, I begin to wonder if I imagined it... and if so, if that's actually for the best. I must not forget that I hate him... right?

Tired from all the work, I decide to do something fun on the weekend, so when Saturday comes, I call my friend Peach and tell her we need to go mushroom hunting if I'm to keep my sanity.

"There's a forest in Connecticut," she replies cheerfully. "I've been meaning to scout it for months."

"Perfect." I locate my hiking boots. "You've got yourself a date."

———

As I gear up for the trip with Peach, I get a call from Pearl.

"It's official," my clutch mate says giddily. "Atonic is preggers."

Great. I'm going to be a grandma *and* a great-aunt at the same time.

His timing impeccable, Bunny rubs against my leg.

It-that-feeds-me should be careful when handling those kittens. They may just inherit their father's craving... for tasty eyeballs.

"Wow," I say into the phone. "Anything I can do to help?"

"Like what?" Pearl asks.

"Pay alimony in Fancy Feast?"

"I'll take some cat food coupons if you've got them."

Huh. That's easy. I have a ton in my collection. "Anything else?"

"Maybe you could help find good homes for the little ones?"

"Sure. I'm going to see my friend Peach today, and I'll ask if she wants one."

"The mycologist?"

"Yep."

"Doesn't she have a pet already?"

I snort. "I don't think mushrooms count."

"Plants can be pets. My friend in L.A. considers her cactus a pet."

I can't help but channel Peach as I say professorially, "Mushrooms aren't a part of the plant kingdom. They're fungi."

"Potato portabella," Pearl says. "Do let me know if she wants one."

"Will do. Anything else?"

"Yes," she says. "Tell me about your hot boss."

Of course. Pearl is gossip personified. It's a miracle it took her this long to get to this question.

I inform her that there isn't much to tell, but then I do tell her about the pranks Gunther and I pulled on each other.

"When a boy pulls your hair or does a prank, he likes you," Pearl says sagely.

"Only if the boy is five. Trust me, Gunther hates me."

She snorts. "You're going to sleep with him, I just know it. If I'm wrong, I'll give you free cheese for a year."

"You're on. Oh, and this is officially the cheesiest bet we've ever made."

———

"No," Peach says when I broach the kitten subject a mile into our hike. "There will not be demon spawn at my house."

Oops. Something I forgot to mention to Pearl is that Peach doesn't like Bunny. She once got me a planter with mushrooms, and Bunny clawed them to shreds, for fun.

"Let me know if you change your mind," I say and look around.

This Connecticut forest was a great idea. Nothing releases the tension from a corporate job in the concrete jungle like an immersion into greenery.

I spot a patch of orange color on the ground to my left. When I bend over, it turns out to be mushrooms—as I thought.

I pick one up and sniff it. Vaguely apricotty.

I extend my catch to Peach. "Chanterelle, right?"

She nods approvingly. "Delicious. Get them all."

I do that, and we continue hunting.

"Are those poisonous?" I ask Peach when I spot small reddish-brown mushrooms with green stains.

Peach checks out my find and whistles. "That's *Psilocybe caerulipes*."

I stare at her with an exasperated expression. "You think that answers my question?"

She plucks the mushrooms and presses a finger into one. It bruises blue. "They're also known as the Little Bluefoot."

I roll my eyes. "Any relation to The Little Bluebeard, the famous mushroom who murdered all his wives?"

Wait, why am I giving her this idea? If fungi could get married, she'd elope with one faster than you can say "cremini."

Peach plucks more of the fungi in question and begins washing them. "Ever hear of magic mushrooms?"

Oh, wow. Edible mushrooms are a great deal as-is, but to find free drugs—that's another level.

I examine the mushrooms appreciatively. "How much are these on the black market?"

She shrugs. "Shrooms are ten bucks per gram or so. But before you get any ideas—they're highly illegal."

"Sure, but—"

I don't finish my sentence because Peach pops a little bit of the Little Bluefoot into her mouth.

"What are you doing?" I demand, shocked.

"Getting high?" She extends some to me.

I gape at the offer. "You want to trip in the forest?"

She shrugs. "Why not? Why else would these little guys produce a substance that binds with receptors in our brains? They *want* us to experience the majesty of the forest the way they do."

I take a step back. "What about the whole illegal bit?"

"You can only get into trouble if caught selling or in possession of them."

I warily accept her offering. "Isn't using them illegal too?"

"How would you get caught? Common drug tests don't bother looking for this drug, and even if they did, your body metabolizes the fun ingredients within twenty-four hours. The only way to tell after that is to do a specialized test on your hair, and even that will only show within ninety days. In any case, that test is rarely used because it's costly and unreliable."

I grin despite myself. Once again, if it has anything to do with fungi, Peach is like a walking Wikipedia. If it turns out that the cure for cancer comes from a mushroom, Peach will be the one to discover it, for sure.

"This is your only chance," she says. "If we take them with us, we'll risk getting into trouble."

"Evil," I mutter. "You know I can't resist an LTO."

She cocks her head. "An LTO?"

"Limited time offer," I say and put a piece of mushroom into my mouth.

As I chew, I frown. The mushroom tastes like flour. Weird.

Swallowing, I look around. "I don't feel any different."

"It might take a half hour or so," she says. "Let's forage in the meantime."

As we resume the mushroom hunt, the conversation turns to my new job, and I tell her what's been happening with me and Gunther, as well as Pearl's thoughts on the matter.

"I have to agree with Pearl," Peach says when I'm done. "It's only a matter of time until the two of you get it on."

Grr. Of course, she'd side with Pearl. They share the

bond of people whose names start with the word "pea" —plus they barter cheese for mushrooms and vice versa.

Whatever. A nearby oak catches my attention. When I turn to it, I see an odd glow—a shimmer of sorts, with pretty colors, all very pleasant to look at.

"Has the shiitake finally hit the fan?" I hear Peach ask in the distance.

The oak looks at her disapprovingly.

"I know," I tell the oak. "It's rude to interrupt a conversation."

Peach grins. "Interrupt your conversation… with a tree?"

"I am Groot," the oak says sternly.

Hmm. That sounds like copyright infringement. I turn away from the oak—and spot a blue jay.

"Hey, little birdy," I say. "I'm sure glad you're not a Mockingjay."

"Yo," the bird replies. "Whazzup?"

I chuckle. "You know, I have a sister named Blue. Ironically, she'd be deathly afraid of you."

The bird hops around. "She watching?"

Hmm. She's usually watching everything through cameras, but this is a forest. Only the spirits are watching us now. I feel connected to them somehow. Connected to every being, every root and branch.

Speaking of connectedness, I didn't come on this trip alone.

Where's Plum? Or was it Apricot?

I turn and spot whatever-her-name-is holding a small frog in her palms.

Sure. That's logical.

She gives it a peck.

I hold my breath, fully expecting the creature to turn into a prince, or maybe The Artist Formally Known as Prince.

Alas, no. Froggie shines with bright colors but stays an amphibian.

Hey, I can't blame Nectarine for trying. With her lack of a love life, it was worth a shot.

Oh, well. I continue to explore the mythical forest with my newly heightened senses.

"Do you taste cotton candy in the air?" my tripmate asks.

I sniff with my mouth. "No. Everything tastes like even numbers to me. Specifically, like forty-two."

She whistles. "That *is* a tasty-sounding number."

I nod, then start a chat with a pine—about life, the universe, and everything.

"That was deep," says either the prickly tree or the fuzzy fruit. "You should be writing some of this down."

Great idea. I pull out my phone and gasp. It's got a strong aura—like that of all the living things. The downside to the aura is that the notes app is difficult to locate, so I decide I'll just leave myself a voicemail with all of my genius ideas.

Yep. Many are related to coupons, so it would be a shame to miss out.

Suddenly, I'm sitting in a meadow, the phone in my hand.

How long was I dictating those ideas?

No clue.

I hang up and locate my friend whose name finally returns to me... assuming it's really Peach, of course.

"Are you Peach?" I ask solemnly.

She stops chewing (or was it talking to?) a chanterelle mushroom. "Aren't we all Peach?"

Are we? No way. I am something sweet, but not a peach.

Molasses, maybe? Maple syrup?

A bee passes by, and for a moment, I experience the world as the little creature—the ultraviolet colors of the flowers, the feeling of moving air on my antennae, the sensation of nectar regurgitation.

Wait a second.

That's my name.

Honey.

Whew.

Content, I lie on my back and examine the limitless sky—which is when my magical trip starts in earnest.

———

"It's getting dark," Peach says some unknown time later.

"Shit. Right." I look around, feeling a lot more normal but still not a hundred percent. "How did we get here?"

She shrugs. "Let's see if I can find us a way back."

She does, thanks to all that foraging experience.

On the ride home, we're subdued, and that night, my sleep is deep and restful. By Sunday morning, I feel completely like myself again—which is when I call Peach.

"Were you as high as I was?" I ask after we exchange awkward hellos.

"Oddly, yes," she says.

"Oddly?"

"The mushroom species we took are considered mild," she says. "It seems we imbibed an overachiever."

"Wow. I shudder to think what a strong shroom would do to me."

"Yeah. To that end, I was wondering... Do you have the mushrooms we collected on our outing?"

I look around.

Nope.

All I find is my disgruntled-looking cat.

It-that-feeds-me needs to justify its pathetic excuse for existence and, well, actually FEED ME. Do not make me collect my pound of human flesh.

I check the fridge. No mushrooms here. I grab a can of cat food and set it up the way Bunny likes—on the counter.

It-that-feeds-me gets to keep those eyelids one more day.

"I don't see any here," I report to Peach.

"Nor here," she says. "The *morel* here is: don't do drugs."

Yeah. Losing free mushrooms is the only reason to

not do drugs. Things like talking to trees and kissing frogs do not count.

"Anyway, enjoy the rest of your Sunday," she says. "Unless you want to go on another mushroom hunt with me today?"

"Can't," I say. "I have to take my work-appropriate attire to the dry cleaners."

———

I've barely started my work on Monday when Gunther walks into my office with an unreadable expression on his cleanshaven face, though his green eyes glow ominously.

"I was under the impression that the pranks were over," he says, omitting the usual morning greetings.

"Well, yeah," I say. "And if this is you starting one, it's a dumb one."

He waves his phone in front of my face. "Care to explain?"

"It's a smartphone?"

He scoffs and presses an icon on his screen.

As soon as I hear my voice emanating from the phone speaker, I realize I'm in trouble.

"Honey Hyman's amazing ideas while on the Little Bluefoot," my voice says cheerfully.

That would be bad enough, but my voice keeps going.

"Idea one: Timber—a dating app for trees."

Nine

SHIT. I'VE REALLY FUCKED UP.

"I can explain," I blurt.

His expressive eyebrow curves. "Explain your use of narcotics? I'd love to hear it."

Damn it. I was going to say that the Little Bluefoot is a brand of vodka, and that I was just drunk.

I take in a calming breath. "Am I fired?"

And if I am, does that mean jail? Also, why am I almost as worried about not seeing Gunther again as I am about jail?

He shrugs. "I haven't decided yet."

"In my defense, I ate it on the weekend," I mutter. "I wasn't high on company time."

He scoffs. "*That* is the best excuse you can come up with?"

"Now look," I say, beginning to get annoyed—my default setting when it comes to Gunther. "It's not like I do drugs on a regular basis. My friend and I were just foraging for mushrooms and happened to find the Little Bluefoot—so we ate some of it."

He rolls his eyes—and he must be the only human in existence to pull off making that look sexy. "Yeah, that's *very* logical. What if it were a poisonous mushroom?"

"My friend is an expert on such things. I'm much more likely to eat a poisonous turducken in her presence."

He doesn't look convinced. "Let's say you found a suitcase with cocaine instead of shrooms—would you use that too?"

I shrug. "Probably not. I've seen enough movies like *True Romance* to know that suitcases like that usually come attached to mobsters."

"Oh? That's the only reason?"

Grr. It's hard to argue when your opponent is in the right—and is as distractingly hot as this one.

I loudly sigh. "Okay, *Mom*. Drugs are bad. Can I get back to work now?"

He cocks his head, a smirk tugging at his full lips. "Are you sure you don't want to hear some of your genius ideas?"

Before I can refuse, he taps the screen once more and, lo and behold, my slightly slurred speech is back, with the following pearl:

"Idea number twenty-seven is for another Munch & Crunch coupon. A sweet kiss from Gunther Ferguson for free if you buy a jar of his signature honey. Idea number twenty-eight—make a cast of Gunther's lips, then make lipstick into that shape... and sell with a BOGO coupon. Idea number twenty-nine—forget the lipstick. Make a towel hanger based on a cast of his—"

He taps the screen again. "You get the idea."

I can feel my cheeks becoming the shade of a stop sign. "I vaguely recall thinking up coupon-related ideas," I say in a choked voice. "At least I had work on my mind."

His smirk turns extra wicked. "If you had work on your mind, why did so many of your ideas involve pimping me out?" With mock seriousness, he adds, "Just to set the record straight, I'd like to keep access to any of my body parts out of the company coupon system, and Buzz Beerin too."

Would I feel better if I fell through the floor— maybe all the way to the lobby?

With a chuckle, Gunther strides out of my office, leaving me to wonder how I'll ever live this down.

And then my phone pings.

It's a text from Gunther.

How about one more idea from your list?

Before I can reply with, "No, thanks," he sends one:

Declare a National Mushroom Day—which would be like Halloween, but everyone would dress like fungi.

Is that really my idea? That sounds like something Peach would come up with.

Shoot me now.

———

As usual, when Gunther leaves to go somewhere—in this case, presumably to get lunch—I'm tempted to set up a prank in his office.

I stop myself, as difficult as it is.

Shit. I need another outlet for this pent-up sexual energy.

Which is when it hits me. I have access to that luxurious and *free* gym, and I haven't used it once.

Well, no time like the present.

I grab a snack in the pantry and take the elevator ride down.

The gym is as ritzy as my first impression of it, to the point where they provide me with free workout clothes and footwear—all new, as well as a free locker to keep it all in.

I'm positively drooling.

Once I've changed into the pricey, brand-name leggings and sports bra and come out into the gym area, my head spins from the many options at my disposal. To keep my sanity, I decide to try a little bit of everything, starting with some free weights because I've read that they're very good for bone density.

I walk up to a bench press and look around for a professional trainer.

None are near, which may be for the best. I want to know whether this will firm up my boobs.

I'd better just try it and see.

Hmm. What's a reasonable weight to bench press for someone my size?

A puny dude who seems weaker than I am is lifting

a bar with a twenty-five-pound weight on each side, so I figure I should be able to do ten without any issues.

I put the tens on and lie down.

Here goes.

I lift the barbell.

It's heavier than I expected.

I slowly lower it down, then push up.

Huh. This is way, way heavier than I expected, but it feels good to work these boob muscles. I didn't even know I had them.

Just to be safe, I will do only one more rep. This is my first time, after all.

I lower the bar to my chest.

Then I start to push it up... but the thing doesn't budge.

Shit.

I strain—but my only accomplishment is that I roll the bar off my chest and onto my neck.

Uh-oh. My breathing was already labored. Now it's completely cut off.

I start to wriggle and even attempt a scream—except nothing comes out.

Fuck.

Is this really how I'm going to die? They'll give me one of those Darwin Awards—like that naked couple a cab driver found dead in 2007. Turns out, they'd decided to have sex on the roof of a high-rise and tumbled down, thus taking themselves out of the gene pool while in the process of reproduction.

Suddenly, strong hands grab the bar and lift it off of me.

As I gulp in air, it smells masculine, with hints of beeswax and smoke.

Blinking, I take in my hero—in all his tank-top-clad, delectable-muscles-glistening-from-sweat glory.

It's Gunther, of course.

It wasn't lunch he went for, but a workout.

Seriously. Shoot me now.

Ten

He's glowering at me, his face thunder dark.

"What were you thinking?" He clanks the bar onto its holders.

"I wanted to work my boob muscles," I mutter as I sit up, my mind muddled by a lack of oxygen and the Gunther-scented air that's replaced it.

He drops to one knee next to the bench and examines my neck with angrily narrowed eyes.

Yes! I've always wanted to play doctor with him.

"You'll have a bruise," he announces.

I wince and rub my throat. "I didn't expect this to happen."

"I fucking hope not," he grumbles, then frowns. "Are you sure you're not still high?"

I shake my head, then realize something. "You just broke your own rule about cuss words!"

He ignores my accusation. "Swear it," he orders.

I put my hand on my chest. "If I'm high, may I never

get free shipping again, or even a ten-percent-off discount."

His expression softens slightly. "From now on, you'll work out with me."

Work out with him? As in, see him in that outfit on a regular basis?

Maybe I *am* still high? Can hallucinogens take one on a sexy trip?

"I mean it," he says, clearly misunderstanding my discombobulated expression. "You've lost the privilege of using the gym by yourself."

His words make me bristle. "It was just ten pounds."

"Oh, really? That bar weighs forty-five pounds, and you had the ten-pound weights on each side. By my math, that's sixty-five pounds."

"Okay, that *is* kind of heavy," I say sheepishly. "I once failed to lift a fifty-pound baby bison."

His forehead creases. "Where did you find a baby bison?"

I rub my throat again and realize it's feeling a lot better. "My parents own a farm. Buffalo Wing was born to a pregnant bison that they'd rescued."

He eyes me with evident fascination. "Was it fun? Growing up on the farm, I mean. Not lifting livestock."

I snort. "In that it was like growing up in a zoo— and that's just thanks to my seven sisters."

His lips finally curve into a hint of a smile. "I had a cat and a younger brother, and even *that* sometimes felt like a zoo."

I sit straighter. "You like cats?"

He sighs. "I've been too busy to get one after moving out on my own, but it's on my to-do list."

"Nice," I say, and resist asking if this means he'd be willing to become an adoptive father to my homicidal maniac. That is, on the off chance an apocalypse comes, and he and I marry in order to save our species.

He checks out my neck again and frowns. "Are you feeling any better?"

"I'm fine," I say, and it's almost true.

"Go change then, and I'll walk you back to your office." The sentence is more of a command than a suggestion.

I eye the equipment around us and pout in disappointment. "I don't get to work out at all? This was my first exercise."

"I'll make you a deal," he says. "If you're feeling okay by tomorrow, I'll show you how to do the bench press properly."

Wow.

His promise is all I can think about as I change, and as he leads me back to our floor.

It's also the only thing on my mind as I finish the day and go home.

Even in my dreams, there's sweaty exercise involving Gunther—but that which works the muscles of my pelvic floor.

―――――

Since I *am* fine the next day, I find myself back in the gym, waiting for Gunther by the evil bench.

Hmm. Why is my heart racing so prematurely? Does it think I've already done some cardio?

Before I can figure it out, Gunther approaches—and makes the situation even worse because he's wearing the same flattering outfit as he did yesterday.

"What's that?" I point at the thin bar he's holding—because that's better than drooling over his physique.

He swaps out the bar that almost killed me, explaining, "This is a woman's bar. It's lighter and thinner—easier for you to grip."

"That sounds sexist," I mutter. "Like you're saying my delicate hands can't handle something that yours can."

He sighs. "That's what they're called—a man's or woman's Olympic bar."

I scoff. "Everyone says things like 'man up' or 'grow a pair,' but that doesn't make such things sound any less sexist."

"Touché. Should we call it the thinner versus thicker bar? Or maybe lighter versus heavier?"

I scratch my chin, exaggerating my thoughtfulness. "Not sure which would be better for the oversensitive ego of the *man's* bar. If we say he's a 'heavier' bar, we may give him a body image problem. And 'thicker' has those phallic overtones that might—"

He rolls his eyes. "We'll go with lighter versus heavier. Now," he adds, his tone a lot more commanding. "Lie down on the bench."

I do as I'm told—and get flashbacks to last night's dream where he also ordered me to lie down before things also got heavy.

"I'm going to spot you," he says.

I blink up at him, more than a little distracted by the fact that his crotch is the closest it's ever been to my face. And in those gym shorts, there's more than a hint of a bulge. With effort, I drag my thoughts out of the gutter. "What does that mean?"

He crouches so that his hands are near my elbows. "If you can't lift it yourself, I'll help you, like this." He gives my elbows a feathery touch.

Holy Arnold Schwarzenegger's overdeveloped manboob muscles. The zing from his touch zooms around my body until it settles somewhere around the stud in my clit.

Suddenly, I feel powerful. Ready for anything.

"I'll lift it now," I state, my voice hoarse.

"That's the spirit," he says with enthusiasm. "Get angry at the weight."

I'm not sure if I'm angry at it, but I push the bar like it's blocking my way into Walmart on Black Friday.

Whoosh.

I get it up—the bar, I mean.

"One," Gunther says, still radiating high energy. "Just make your movements slower. More controlled."

I was going to be slow and controlled on the way down anyway—the last thing I want is to drop this thing. When I push the weight back up again, I go slow too and see why he suggested I do it. This way, I actually feel the muscles I'm supposed to be exercising.

"Two," he says.

"The lighter bar is easier to work with," I admit.

"Don't talk," he says. "Focus on your breathing. Exhale as you lift up."

I shut up and do as he ordered—and feel the difference.

"Five, six, seven, eight," he counts, and when I get to fifteen, he tells me to stop.

"Great job," he says. "Are you sure you've never done bench press before?"

My chest flushes for some reason—probably with pride.

Gunther looks at my exposed skin with approval.

Wow. I do one set of bench press, and my boobs are irresistible?

"You've got the pump," he says.

"What?" I check out my feet in case one of my sneakers has sprouted a stiletto heel—or has grown pipes to pump water.

"The pump is what we call it when your muscles look plump after exercise." He puts his arm into the classic flexing position and blows up his bicep like a sexy meat balloon.

I'm speechless. Is he illustrating his words with that maneuver or trying to make me ovulate?

"I don't think 'plump' is the right word for your bicep," I say when I trust myself to speak without drooling.

A smirk appears on his full lips. "Since you're the language police today, you tell me a better word."

"Engorged." Am I still talking about his bicep?

"Fine. 'The pump' is when your muscles look *engorged.* It happens after you push your muscles to the limit and blood rushes to that area. People who work out enjoy seeing their muscles look bigger, even if only temporarily."

Uh-huh. My mind must still be rolling in filth because I'm thinking of another scenario that involves blood flow in order to look bigger—also associated with the word "engorged."

"Your pectorals even got flushed," he continues, "which is rare." He glances approvingly at my chest. "I'm actually jealous. As you're about to see, my chest doesn't get flushed, even when I get the pump."

"Wait. You're doing bench press also?" And can I witness it without throwing myself at him, pussy first?

"Don't worry," he says. "You don't need to spot me."

"Oh?" Who's going to spot *me* from dropping my panties?

"The weight I'm going to do is much too heavy for you to help with," he explains. "And I'm not being sexist. Few men here could spot me either."

As if to demonstrate, he stacks enough weights on the bar that if you put them on a giant seesaw, they'd probably send an elephant flying—and I'm not talking about Dumbo.

"Is that all?" I ask with noticeable snark in my voice. He's clearly showing off.

He frowns at the weights. "You're right. I haven't accounted for the weight of the lighter bar." He walks over to a nearby rack and grabs two itsy-bitsy five-pound weights to add on each side of his monstrosity.

I watch in fascination as he lies down, inhales enough air to blow up a birthday balloon, and lifts the bar in a smooth, steady motion.

Fuck me.

The ends of the bar bend from all that punishing gravity, yet Gunther's arms lower the whole thing down, push up again, and repeat the same Herculean feat fifteen times. On the last few reps, he grunts gutturally, generating pornographic fantasies of him coming, emptying himself inside me after a rough, pounding session, and—

"How was my form?" he asks out of nowhere.

Shit. He's already up from the bench and looking at me like I'm crazy.

And I am. How else do I explain that last train of thought?

I clear my throat. "You went up and down pretty smoothly." I pointedly look at his chest. "And there's that pump."

Would it be that inappropriate to lick just one bead of sweat from his chest? What about his face?

"Your turn," he says bossily as he removes all the weights.

I lie down—and there's that heart-rate-spiking bulge proximity again. I'm getting so acquainted with it, I might as well give his cock a name.

Maybe Mr. Suck & Lick? Reminiscent of Munch & Crunch, but with no cannibalistic overtones.

"You got it," Gunther says with maniacal energy. "Go ahead and get angry at that weight."

Angry—no. Horny—yep.

I channel whatever I've got and lift the bar on an out breath.

"There you go," Gunther praises. "Now give me fourteen more just like that."

If he were this good at motivating me upstairs, I'd be the hardest worker in corporate history. I get to the count of fifteen, and he only needs to help my elbows a little on the last rep—and that (or all the blood flow to my boob muscles) makes my head spin for a second as I sit up.

He examines me worriedly. "Are you okay?"

I bob my now-steady head.

"Want to do one more set after this? Three is a good number."

I manage another nod. "Now it's your turn."

He grins, adds even more weights, and lies down.

His face is sexy when he's under all that strain, all manly and rugged, kind of like a lumberjack's.

Grr. To distract myself from impure thoughts, I mimic his motivational counting—which is easy because I'm genuinely excited by what he's doing, just in the wrong way.

"Fourteen... fifteen!" I exclaim as another orgasmic grunt bursts from his tightly pressed lips. "Great job."

Whew. I'm actually happy to do my set. If I'm lucky,

it'll burn off some of this twitchy energy I've got coursing through me.

Nope. Even after two more sets, the feeling of pump is not exclusive to my chest. It's also in my lady bits.

"Ready for flies?" he asks.

"Ready for what?" Is this some joke pertaining to my name, i.e. like flies to honey?

"Flies is a type of exercise." He gestures at a nearby machine that looks like a torture rack.

Seeing my skeptical expression, he sits on the seat in front of the crisscross contraption, grabs the handles attached to it, and pulls until his hands meet in front of his chest.

Oh, my. At the end of the motion, his pecs flex hard and look incredibly huge... and very lick-inspiring.

Okay. I get it now. The fly in the name of this exercise is a reference to the Spanish Fly—the alleged aphrodisiac that makes women feel hot and bothered, the way I am right now.

"See?" he says as he performs the next rep. "This movement is like the flapping of wings."

"Sure. Wings of an albatross, not a fly."

He arches an eyebrow as his hands come together again. "First, I think there was a compliment in there somewhere. Second, who said anything about *Musca domestica*?"

I roll my eyes. "Musca domestica?"

He does another rep. "That's the scientific name for the house fly. Since you've confused the creature with the verb, I thought I'd be more precise for you."

"Don't talk," I say in my best imitation of his voice. "Focus on your breathing. Exhale as you fly up."

He grins. "This isn't actually my weight. I was just showing you what to do with whatever was on." He reaches over and moves the little pin from the weights attached to the torture device all the way down. "Now I'll feel a challenge," he boasts, then does the same movement again—still pretty effortlessly, with all the weights going for a ride and his tempting lips pressed into a firm line.

As before, I keep myself distracted by counting for him. Midway through his set, I feel the hair on the back of my neck stand up, like someone has walked over my grave.

I turn and see the cause—Tiffany. She's on an elliptical machine, giving me the evil eye.

I pretend not to notice her and wait for Gunther to finish.

As I plop my butt onto the torture machine and push the handles in front of my chest, Gunther frowns. "You're not controlling it." He leans in. "Grip the handles tight." He clasps his big hands around mine and gives my fingers a gentle squeeze—presumably to illustrate what he means.

My strong, primal reaction to that instruction makes me wish this place gave out a change of panties to go with the workout clothes.

"Now push, like this." He brings my hands forward slowly.

I try not to faint as the demonstration continues.

"At the end, flex down there." He points at a spot just below my clavicle.

I flex where he said to, even though what I really want to do is cross my legs and flex some other muscles altogether.

"Good job," he says and starts counting for me—and I could swear I'm developing a fetish for numbers between one and fifteen.

"I don't think you should do any more," Gunther says when I'm done with my flies.

I frown. "Why? You think I'm too delicate?" Because I have enough energy for double the weightlifting I've done… followed by a hard and fast ride on Mr. Suck & Lick after that.

"I'm sure you could handle it," he says reassuringly.

Weightlifting or the cock? "Yeah? Then why stop?"

He sighs. "A common mistake beginners make is going too hard, and then they're much too sore the next day. That discourages them from coming back."

"How sore will I get?" I dart a glance at his bulge.

"I've seen some who couldn't walk the next day," he says. Seeing my eyes widen, he quickly adds, "That was after leg day—and in any case, this all hurts less as you practice more. And stretch."

I moisten my lips. "I'm willing to put in the time… and I'm very stretchy."

His emerald eyes gleam. "That's a great attitude. Make sure to always eat well an hour before and after."

I swallow all the excess saliva. "Satiate hunger before an epic session? How very practical."

He wipes a bead of sweat off his chest. "Make sure to hydrate well too."

"Good idea." I *have* been losing exuberant amounts of moisture... in *all* the places.

"Okay," he says. "To complete today, how about a steam room?"

My mouth goes slack as I picture us in said steam room, all his hard-as-a-rock flesh, more of those beads of sweat adorning said flesh, all the massages he'd offer to soothe my aching muscles, all the—

"See you?" He looks confused—probably because of the drooling expression on my face.

"Yeah. See you!"

I rush to the locker room like a maniac, which is where I stumble into Tiffany.

"I saw the two of you," she says nastily at me.

"And?"

"And you're being a cliché," she says.

I arch an eyebrow.

"You know what I mean." She slams the door of her locker. "Sleeping with the boss to advance your career."

My eyeroll is imbued with the same attitude it had back when we were in high school. "What career? I'm here for the coupon project, and that's it. But I find it interesting how quickly your mind jumped to that very specific idea."

She sucks in air for a rebuttal, but I don't bother to wait for it and step over to my locker instead.

To my relief, Tiffany doesn't follow.

Opening my locker, I strip, cover myself with a towel, and sprint in search of the steam room.

When I locate it, I can taste my disappointment all the way down to my clit.

Gunther isn't in the steam room.

He can't be, not without breaking major societal taboos. Being attached to the women's locker room, the steam room isn't coed—something I would've realized if my mind weren't fogged by out-of-control hormones.

Oh, well. I take advantage of the steam room anyway, then finally take what I desperately need at this point—a cold shower.

·

Eleven

THE NEXT DAY, I FIND IT HARD TO CONCENTRATE IN THE morning. My chest is sore from the prior day's exercise, and my private bits are sore because I might've overused my vibrator to the fantasies of a much naughtier version of that workout.

Somehow, I manage to get something done, but just as I enter focus mode, Gunther's head pops into my office. "Want to do shoulders with me today?"

My heart leaps. "Is the Mother Pope overprotective of her cubs?"

He grins. "I'll take that weird reply as a yes."

———

When it comes to sexual frustration, watching Gunther work his shoulders is worse for my libido than our workout yesterday. The following day is even more trying because he works his legs. Yet even that is nothing compared to when we train our back muscles the day after, and the most frustrating of all the workouts has to be the day he flexes his big, strong, need-to-be-touching-me arms.

And so, for the next few weeks, we go to the gym together by day, and I masturbate excessively by night. The latter becomes so varied that I run out of ideas and end up visiting "Pet the Petunia"—a blog my clutch mate Lemon runs.

Turns out, I'm a fan of a technique dubbed "Live Long and Prosper." It's the one where your fingers are held in the V-shape of the Vulcan salute.

———

I'm sitting in my office and fanning myself after my latest workout with Gunther when Ashildr walks in, holding a festive Hallmark card.

"It's Tiffany's birthday," he says. "Can you sign this for her?"

Great. Tiffany has been giving me the stink eye whenever our paths cross, and now I have to find something nice to say to her. Maybe I should go with: "I wish for you to get wiser in your advancing age. You're too much of a dumb asshole right now." Or: "May you have positivity in your life. It might be the only way to wipe that cunty sourpuss expression off your face."

Out of the corner of my eye, I see Gunther walking to his office, and that gives me an idea. Maybe I could say something like: "May your wishes come true—unless they involve Mr. Suck & Lick, in which case I hope you shrivel up and die."

No. Can't.

With a sigh, I write, "Congrats," followed by a scribble of my name that I hope she doesn't recognize.

Just as I hand Ashildr the marker back, a droplet of red liquid appears on the white of the paper.

A droplet of blood.

Time seems to slow, and I feel my senses leave my body as I stare at the droplet being joined by another, then another, all escaping Ashildr's left nostril.

"Are you okay?" I hear Ashildr say, his voice coming at me as though I were at the bottom of a well. "Why do you look so pale?"

There's a clamor. I think it's my office door—but it could be the sound of my consciousness fleeing.

Just like that, my eyes roll into the back of my head, and I pass out.

Twelve

I blink open my eyes and find myself in Gunther's strong arms. He's kneeling on the floor, his touch electrifying wherever our bodies meet.

I close my eyes again and wonder if I'm having that dream—the one where Gunther uses me to work his biceps. If so, why am I not in the air? Has he set me down to rest? All I know is that being at the gym would explain why I'm feeling so damned lightheaded. I must've used too much weight on the last set.

"She's just come to," Ashildr's voice says from a distance. "I think."

Oh, fuck. This might not be a dream.

It all comes flooding back. Ashildr started bleeding, and I swooned like a ninny—and Gunther must've seen it.

I keep my eyes firmly shut now. The last thing I want is to see Ashildr's nosebleed again and pass out a second time. Just thinking about the cursed situation makes me woozy.

"Can you guys leave?" I whisper. "I need all the oxygen." If I'm lucky, there's no blood anywhere in my office.

"Leave us." The commanding tone with which Gunther barks out the two words would make a military commander proud.

"Feel better," Ashildr mumbles, and then I hear him scatter away.

I peek through my eyelashes.

Whew. He took the card, his nose, and all signs of blood away. Now if I can get rid of Gunther, I might not die of humiliation after all.

"How do you feel?" Gunther asks softly.

I feel like an idiot. The first time I heard Ashildr tell me about his dry nose situation, I should've gotten a humidifier for my office.

"That's it." Gunther picks me up from the floor like a bride—or a pair of dumbbells. "Let's go."

As he starts to carry me, I instinctively clutch his shoulders, then realize what I'm doing and wiggle in his arms, but his grip is like iron shackles.

And now I've got kink on my mind.

"Where are you taking me?" I demand, doing my best not to inhale too much of his yummy scent that surrounds me.

"The hospital." By the time he states this, we're midway to the elevators.

A hospital is a place where I might come across the

sight of more blood, so taking me there would be like trying to cure alcoholism with Spirytus Stawski—a Polish vodka that's ninety-six-percent alcohol.

"Put me down." I wiggle futilely again, pushing on his rock-hard shoulder muscles.

Despite my loud demand, every single Munch & Crunch minion around us has their nose buried in their screen, acting as though the sight of Gunther carrying a belligerent female coworker is as mundane as a case of the Mondays.

"Seriously, I'm fine," I growl when we're by the elevator.

He presses me tighter against his chest to push the elevator button with his elbow. "People who are fine don't pass out."

Should I tell him the truth?

No way. That's the last thing I want. He'll either mock or pity me, and I'm not sure which would be worse.

"My sugar must've dropped," I blurt.

Oops. That was clearly the wrong excuse. His eyes are like a magnifying glass pointed at a bug on a sunny day. "You forgot to eat... again?"

Again? Oh, right. The day when I thought we almost kissed, I used this same excuse.

Shit. After that incident, he was bugging me to eat for a while. What's worse, since we've been exercising together, he's been lecturing me about proper caloric intake after workouts—and often shares his protein shakes with me.

Time to backpedal. "It's an honest mistake. I just got busy. When you—"

"Don't," he snaps, then gently sets me down.

Am I going to be the first person in the world to get fired for not eating? Or the first employee to get spanked next to the elevator?

Gunther pulls out a protein bar from his suit jacket's inner pocket. "Bite this."

Swallowing a "bite me," I do as he says and groan internally at the intensity with which he watches me— like he doesn't trust me to swallow.

I chew very pointedly and gulp it down loudly. Then, for good measure, I open my mouth to show him the morsel is really gone.

His eyes gleam. "Good. Now we're going to the cafeteria."

The elevator opens just as I ask, "Why?"

He herds me inside. "Because a cafeteria is a type of room where you can eat?"

I grunt. "Octothorpe, disable annoying Wikipedia definitions."

To my shock, a small speaker above my head says in a chipmunk voice, "All notifications are already disabled in the elevator."

"Great," I grumble. "The coffee machine doesn't have AI, but the elevator does. I fear to talk to a toilet."

Gunther presses the cafeteria button, a tiny smile tugging at his lips.

I put my hands on my hips. "You never answered my question."

He sighs. "Since you forget to eat, I'm going to supervise you."

My hands drop to my sides. "What?"

"We'll have lunch together. Eat using actual plates. It's a foreign concept, I know."

I roll my eyes. "And what, you're going to handfeed me?" I'm glad I didn't lie about forgetting my other basic bodily functions. He's clearly itching for more things he can supervise.

Gunther's smirk is downright dastardly. "Handfeeding is the last resort."

Hmm. Why does the idea sound a little hot?

No. Snap out of it. This isn't okay.

Or is it? I have been getting tired of all the pantry food—even if it's free. Speaking of... "Are we going to talk business as we eat?"

"Why?" he asks, mimicking my earlier tone.

"Ashildr told me if it's a business meeting, the cafeteria meals are free."

Gunther snorts. "We *can* talk business, but we don't have to. Either way, it's my treat."

"Oh. I guess it's wouldn't be the end of the world to have to eat lobster with you there... just this once."

The elevator opens, and as Gunther strides out, he says over his shoulder, "Not just this once. Every day."

Oh.

Every day. Together.

I don't get a chance to decide how I feel about this development because I have to hurry to keep up with his long strides as he leads me into the ritzy cafeteria, heading right for the most exclusive, enclosed area where they have a hostess, waiters, and laminated menus in a fancy Centeria Script font.

"Hello, Mr. Ferguson," the hostess says, her voice laced with my namesake. "Would you like the meeting table or your personal?"

"Personal," he says.

Nodding, she takes us to the nicest table in the corner—one with utensils that look like they're made of platinum and a view of Manhattan that momentarily renders me mute.

When I snap out of it, I glance at the menu—and mutter curses under my breath when I see the insane prices.

"Language," Gunther chides, but his tone is less stern than usual.

I flip a page. "I thought this place was subsidized."

He shrugs. "The self-serve section is more subsidized. Either way, given that we've stolen a chef from a Michelin-starred restaurant, I'd call these prices reasonable."

"If you say so."

He leans in conspiratorially. "If it makes the deal lover in you feel any better, I'm basically going to be paying myself here."

Ah. Right. I sometimes forget that he owns everything Munch & Crunch, this restaurant included.

"In that case, I'm getting the surf and turf," I say, naming the most expensive item on the menu. "I want to make sure you profit."

"Lucky," he says and waves at the waiter.

Why is that lucky? Before I can ask, the waiter comes with a fancy bread basket.

Gunther orders the surf and turf for me, and an avocado toast and Eggs Benedict for himself.

Two meals? Given what I've seen him do at the gym, that tracks.

"Do you always order off-menu?" I ask when the waiter leaves.

"The toast and eggs are on the brunch menu," Gunther says. "In any case, the chef always keeps the ingredients ready, since I order that combo often."

Hmm. So why am I lucky to be getting steak and lobster? "Are you a vegetarian?"

He shakes his head. "I stick to items that are low in iron."

That's right. He mentioned his condition before, but because the context was donating blood, I blocked it out as I do anything related to my phobia.

Crap. Now that I'm on that train of thought, I feel woozy again.

"Bite the bread," he orders. "You're looking pale again."

With a sigh, I do as I'm told.

The bread is amazing, especially the crispy crust—so it actually does make me feel better.

"You now have a new set of responsibilities at this job," Gunther says when I look back up.

"Oh?"

He grabs a roll from the basket for himself. "You'll

take a picture of your every breakfast and dinner, and text it to me."

My hackles start to rise, but I suppress them. My own lies landed me in this situation. "What if I don't? Are you going to handfeed me?"

"Worse. Every missing picture will cost you one percent of your bonus."

"I'm getting a bonus?"

"As of now, yes." Seeing the interest in my eyes, he looks triumphant. "Or more correctly… maybe."

Fine. I can take some pictures if I get paid for it later. After all, people post this sort of thing on their social media for free.

"What time do you want them?"

The corners of his full lips twitch. "When do you usually eat?"

I tell him, and he nods approvingly. "You can text me right after."

"Sure. We wouldn't want to delay my feedings."

"Something like that."

"Fine. I'll try."

He frowns. "Not try. Do."

"Okay, Yoda."

"If you need an extra reminder, I can text you. But if I do that, I might as well share with you some more of your great mushroom ideas. Like this one." He pulls out his phone and presses a button on the screen.

"Color all road signs purple," my voice says.

I cringe. "Is this blackmail?"

He spreads his hands. "I said I'd only text them to *you*, not to a whole group of people."

Yep. Definitely blackmail.

The waiter shows up with a tray.

I start drooling. Everything looks amazing. My surf and turf is like those fake meals they make for advertisements out of glue, sponges, and shoe polish, except somehow real. Better yet, the culinary masterpiece tastes just as good as it looks—and if the blissed-out expression on Gunther's face is anything to go by, his food is great too.

Is this what Gunther would look like if he were eating me?

I nearly choke on my lobster.

Gunther glowers at me. "I never said to eat so fast that you end up choking."

Would I want him to choke me as he eats me?

Grr. Seriously? I need a distraction, stat, before my face starts matching the lobster on my plate.

"Tell me something about you," I blurt.

Yeah. This is a safer topic—unless he's going to tell me he likes to eat pierced honey pots.

Gunther cocks his head. "Like what?"

I shrug. "Something few people know?"

He opens his mouth, then seems to reconsider whatever he was about to say. Finally, he says, "I'm not sure I can trust you with this."

I all but rub my hands with glee. "Come on. Stop being such a tease."

"Maybe if you told me something embarrassing about you?"

Evil. "You already have the mushroom ideas. What more do you need?"

"Something more personal," he says.

"Fine." I dip a piece of lobster into butter. "I like horror flicks."

It started as an attempt at exposure therapy, but I discovered that the sight of blood on screen doesn't bother me at all—probably because I know that it's really corn or chocolate syrup with red food coloring, or in more recent films, pure CGI.

He looks like he's about to choke on the mushed avocado. "Are you psychic or something?"

"Why?"

"The dirty secret I hesitated to share has to do with horror flicks. Horrible ones."

I squint at him. "No way."

"Yeah. I like those despised 'This vs. That' movies."

I drop my fork with a gasp. "Me too."

He looks dubious. "You're telling me you're the first person I've met who's like me?"

I match his skepticism. "Assuming you're not making this up."

"What is your favorite?" he demands. "Quickly."

"*Freddy vs. Jason*. Yours? Quickly."

"*Alien vs. Predator*," he responds without a moment of hesitation.

"That one is worse than mine—and you said it so

quick. Maybe you're not lying after all. Fuck. I can't believe I've met another 'versus' fan."

His good humor dims. "Language, please."

With an eyeroll, I grab a knife and begin cutting up my steak as Gunther watches me with growing disapproval.

"I'll try not to swear going forward," I say. "Pinky swear."

"It's not just that." He nods at my hands. "The knife should be in your right hand."

"Is that so?"

"That's why it was on the right side of your plate," he says. "And since we're on the subject of table manners, you shouldn't be using the lobster fork for steak." He gestures at the normal fork on the left side of my plate.

There's enough sarcasm in my tone to kill a horse as I ask, "Anything else, dear sir?"

He nods, all dead serious. "The prongs of the fork should face away from you." He takes his fork and knife and pantomimes cutting an imaginary steak.

"Got it." I take the right utensils into the correct appendages and slowly cut the steak as he instructed, rolling my eyes throughout.

"Thank you," he says.

"No problem," I lie. "Now, tell me. What's your least favorite 'vs.' movie you've seen?"

He strokes his chin. "*King Kong vs. Godzilla.*"

"That's not even a horror movie."

"Yeah. Maybe. What about you?"

"If we're talking non-horror, *Scott Pilgrim vs. the World.*"

He gasps theatrically. "That's such an underrated movie. Why is it your least favorite?"

I grin. "It's those positive reviews that are the problem. To be a genuine 'vs.' movie, one has to have cheesy horror and crappy ratings."

His emerald eyes sparkle as he returns my grin. "You've got to admit, though, it had an amazing cast."

"Oh?"

"Totally. One of the evil exes later starred as The Human Torch and later, famously, as Captain America. Another was Superman, and yet another became Captain Marvel."

I try the grilled asparagus that came with my dish—and even the normally boring vegetable tastes like a delicacy here. "Cheater," I say. "I'm getting the sense that you like superhero movies just as much as 'vs.' ones. Or more."

He shakes his head vehemently. "No. 'Vs.' movies will always have a special place in my heart. Still, who doesn't like a good superhero blockbuster?"

"Me." I narrow my eyes at him. "Let me guess. Your favorite is *Captain America*. Chris Evans is a clean-cut goody two-shoes in that franchise—so you obviously can relate."

He looks down at his perfectly tailored suit, then back at me. "That would be like me saying that you must be a fan of *The Girl with the Dragon Tattoo* because the heroine has tattoos and piercings."

I wave my fork triumphantly. "I *do* like that movie, as well as the Swedish versions and the books, so my logic *is* sound."

"Well, my favorite hero is Deadpool. Not so clean cut."

"Sure—played by clean-cut Ryan Reynolds. Just watch *The Proposal*. I rest my case."

He blows out a breath. "You're incorrigible."

"If by that, you mean arguing with me is futile, then yes. Don't even bother." I finally get around to the mashed potatoes, and not surprisingly, they're heavenly. "I can't believe you can tolerate all those bad words that are in *Deadpool*."

He snorts. "Just because I happen to think that dropping F-bombs at work is unprofessional doesn't mean that I'm a prude."

"Doesn't it, though?"

"Nope." He glances at my plate enviously. "How's your iron-rich selection?"

"Delicious," I say sheepishly. "And sorry, next time I can order something else."

"Don't. Let me live vicariously through you."

Huh. "Like this?" Using the correct hand, I stab a piece of steak lithely with my fork, then raise it sensuously to my mouth before chewing slowly.

Wow. He must really, really miss beef. His ravenous eyes remind me of a starving wolf.

Gunther readjusts his tie. "That's more like teasing." For some reason, his voice is a bit hoarse.

"Sorry," I say, but I don't mean it for a second. At the

gym, he teases me with his man meat, so it's only fair I tease him with my cow version.

"Tell me something else about you," Gunther says, pointedly changing the topic.

I eat a morsel of lobster as un-teasingly as I can—going as far as to forego dipping it in butter. "As you already know, I like the Ramones. But also, Sex Pistols. Or should I say Bleep Pistols?"

He cringes. "The Ramones are behind that headache-inducing *Spiderman* song you played in your office?"

"And you dare call yourself a fan of superheroes?" I tsk tsk. "Who's *your* favorite musician?"

He smiles fondly. "Kenny G."

I spit-take my lobster. "The dorky smooth jazz guy?"

"No." His green eyes turn slitted. "The talented musician."

"Let me hear a song of his," I challenge.

Gunther takes out his phone and puts on *something*. At first, I think maybe I'm at Enya's funeral, but then a sad saxophone comes into play, at which point I realize the funeral is for the whole concept of good music.

"Turn that down," I beg.

He lowers the volume until you can barely hear the sax, but it's still too loud.

"All the way down," I say. "And warn your lawyers. My ears will be pressing charges."

"You're insane." Gunther cradles his still-mewing phone protectively. "This is great music."

"Horrible."

"Well, the market has spoken." He finally turns the crime against humanity off. "Kenny G is the best-selling artist of all time, with more than seventy-five million records sold."

"Oh, the bliss that is silence." I wipe non-existent sweat from my brow. "The Ramones basically invented punk rock, as in a whole new genre of music."

"Kenny G redefined Easy Listening."

I snort. "Easy Listening. It should be called Ear Violation."

Gunther opens his mouth to retort, but the waiter comes over and examines our almost-empty plates. "Anyone have room for dessert?"

Gunther and I glance at each other questioningly.

"Want to share something?" I ask.

"I don't usually eat sweets," he says. "But I can have a spoonful of whatever you choose."

"Do you have ice cream?" I ask the waiter.

The waiter straightens his spine. "We have vanilla, chocolate, green tea, and butter pecan."

Wow. "Let us get vanilla," I say and flash a grin at Gunther. "I'm guessing that's your favorite flavor."

Gunther mumbles something unintelligible while the waiter scampers off.

"So, how do you like working at Munch & Crunch?" Gunther asks.

I arch an eyebrow. "Is that a threat? Or are you making sure this *is* a business lunch after all, so you can use it as a tax write-off?"

He huffs. "It would take a lot more than vanilla jokes to get me to threaten you with termination. As to taxes, I—"

"Don't misunderstand me, I'd approve it if you got some money back from the government for this lunch." I make a sweeping gesture at the table. "In your tax bracket, it's probably forty percent off."

He snorts. "Did my accountant put you up to this?"

Before I can retort, the waiter comes back, carrying a fancy tray with ice cream. When we're alone again, I stick my hand into my pocket as I ask, "Mind if I make it a sundae?"

Gunther frowns. "No, but—"

Seeing me pull out a tiny bag of M&Ms, he stops talking and stares as I garnish the ice cream with the candy. Next, I pull out a handful of wrapped caramels, unwrap them, and add them to my creation, followed by a bag of gummy bears.

He finally snaps out of his reverie. "Do you always carry candy in your pockets?"

"Only when I work at a place that offers them for free in the pantry," I say.

"Right, but why not just order a sundae in the first place?"

I look up at him like he's dimwitted. "And pay double?"

"I told you I'm paying."

I shrug. "I don't want anyone to waste money, not even you."

"All righty then." He watches in fascination as I add

a few more pantry items to the dessert, but when I pull out Reese's Pieces, he cringes. "If you're still willing to share, please skip anything to do with peanut butter."

I halt in my tracks. "Are you allergic?"

He nods, but he looks uncertain.

Well, whatever. "The sundae has plenty of ingredients already," I announce with fanfare. "Dig in."

He puts a spoonful into his mouth and hums approvingly. "Not sure if my dentist will love the effects of this, but it tastes great."

I eat a spoonful as well and nod. I might not have the insane sweet tooth of my sister Lemon, but I enjoy an occasional sundae—especially when it's free.

"Do you know why they call it a sundae?" Gunther asks. "With that weird spelling?"

I shake my head. "I've got a feeling some mansplaining is about to commence."

He puts his spoon down. "Not if you don't want to know."

I gobble another spoonful. "Well, you've piqued my curiosity. Why is it called that and spelled that way?"

"Maybe I should leave you hanging."

If our joint gym sessions are anything to go by, he's very good at leaving me hanging—to the point that I have to use Lemon's masturbation blog as a guide. "You know I can use this invention called Google?"

"Don't do that. I'll explain." He licks his spoon. "Back in the day," he starts in a professorial tone, "ice cream sodas were very popular, but there were laws banning them on Sundays so—"

"Wait, why?"

"They tasted so good they were considered sinful."

"Huh. The bar for sinful was clearly pretty low before fried Oreos and Pornhub were invented."

He grins. "Yeah. They had to invent another ice cream dessert that was tamer, and thus more suitable to enjoy on a Sunday. It became associated with the day, but they used a different spelling for it, in reverence for the word 'Sunday.'"

So, by that logic, if Mr. Suck & Lick tastes sinfully good—and there's a good chance he might—I'll have to come up with a tamer version for Sundays. Maybe only lick him through a condom?

"Check, please," Gunther says to the passing waiter, interrupting my lexicographical contemplations. Then he turns to me. "Sorry. I have to run to a meeting."

I gesture at the empty dessert plate. "We were done, so it's all good."

Gunther grabs the check from the waiter and drops a wad of cash on it. "Same time, same place tomorrow?"

"Sure." My treacherous heart speeds up—probably as revenge for all that cholesterol I've just consumed. "Walk back together?" I ask, leaping to my feet.

He steps close to me, eyes regretful. "The meeting is downtown, so I can only accompany you as far as the elevator."

"That works." Seriously, heart, WTF?

The walk to the elevator is somehow awkward—at

least on my end, because I'm feeling the flutter of fluffy kitten paws in my belly. Which reminds me…

"Would you like a kitten?" I blurt.

He slows his pace and turns an incredulous emerald gaze toward me. "A what?"

"A baby cat. You know, tiny, adorable, mewing. Any of that ring a bell?"

"Why?"

I sigh. "You mentioned you liked them, so I've been meaning to ask, but—"

"I mean, why do you have kittens to give away in the first place?"

"Oh. My tomcat defiled my clutch mate's female cat."

He resumes his brisk pace. "That sounds vaguely incestuous."

"That's what I said!"

He holds the cafeteria door for me with a grin. "Also, at the risk of being accused of mansplaining again, I should let you know that the equivalent of tomcat for female cats is *molly.*"

"I'm pretty sure 'molly' is another name for ecstasy, as in the drug MDMA," I say as I pass.

"Just because that drug is called that doesn't mean it can't also be a term for a female cat. Ecstasy has other meanings." He stops by the elevator and very considerately presses both the "down" and "up" buttons.

Watching those fingers, I can easily picture him making me scream in ecstasy—no drugs required.

I clear my suddenly dry throat. "My sister called her female cat a queen."

"That's used in the context of reproduction. The cat birthing process is called a queening—though I'm not sure why."

"You don't know something? The universe might implode." I smile to take the sting out of my words, then add, "Maybe it's because female cats have a stereotype for being fancy and finicky, and so do queens."

"Maybe." The downward-heading elevator opens, and Gunther glances at it, then back at me.

Is it my imagination, or is he reluctant to leave me?

"Bye?" I venture softly.

"Yeah," he says but doesn't move toward the elevator.

"Same time and place tomorrow?" I ask and want to smack myself. Why am I making it sound like a date?

"Yes. Tomorrow," he says, yet he still doesn't move toward the about-to-close elevator.

A new elevator door opens, this one with the "up" light above it—as in, mine.

"I should go," I say, but I stay put.

"Yeah." He steps toward me. "We don't want to be late."

As if in reply, his elevator door closes.

In unison, we reach to press the "down" button.

Fucking hell. His finger touches mine, and it feels as though the stud in my clit has become a component in the elevator motor.

I jerk my hand away.

The "down" door opens again.

All I can think of is him going down on me.

Gunther points at the "up" door as he captures my gaze.

Seriously?

His emerald-green eyes feel as deep as the ocean as his lips mouth, "Go."

I can't, so I come up with, "You go first."

"Ladies first," he says, but the way he looks at me makes me feel like the opposite of a proper lady.

"Age before beauty," I manage to say.

"I'm just a couple of years older," he says huskily, and still doesn't fucking move.

This is ridiculous. He's acting like he did in the pantry—pretending he wants to kiss me when we both know he wants anything but.

"Would it be inappropriate if we hugged goodbye?" I ask, because *something* needs to happen to break this stupid stalemate.

His dark eyebrows furrow.

"Or is there a hug form we need to fill out with HR first?" I say—and that seems to break whatever spell came over him. In an eyeblink, he has me enveloped in his strong arms, pressed against all of his delectably hard parts.

Wow. There's something extra hard in his pocket. Is that—

Before I can finish the thought—or wonder how to spell "huggasm"—Gunther has already let me go and is diving into the elevator car like he's late for an organ transplant.

I stagger into my elevator, but I no longer wish to go back up to my office.

Nope.

What I need is the gym floor since that's the closest cold shower.

Thirteen

When I get home that day, I open the freezer and grab a Munch & Crunch-branded sausage, egg, and cheese burrito.

These were on a BOGO sale, and I got so many I've grown tired of them. With a sigh, I pop the thing into the microwave, and as I wait, I open a fresh can of cat food. This brand and flavor is the only thing my cat deigns to eat, and it just so happens that it never goes on sale.

"Bunny?" I yell.

He waltzes into the room and gracefully leaps onto the counter where I set his bowl.

It-that-feeds-me has assuaged my wrath once again. It should always be eating meals that cost less than mine. And are less nutritious.

My phone rings with a text from Gunther.

It's dinner time, and I haven't gotten what I was promised. Here's a helpful idea from your voicemail—for now only shared between me and you: "Ban all polka dot dresses. Ceramics too. Maybe even the comics with the Polka-Dot Man."

I smack myself on the forehead, which makes Bunny look up grumpily from his bowl.

If It-that-feeds-me wants pain, just ask. My claws and teeth would be eager to oblige.

I take a picture of my sad burrito, send it back to Gunther, and start thinking of a scathing reply to go with it—but my phone rings.

My heart skips.

Is it Gunther?

Nope. It's Pearl.

"If it isn't the cheesiest of my siblings," I say as I take the call.

"Very funny," she says. "How was Gunther today?"

I grin. "Someone wants her nightly gossip fix?"

"You know it. Now dish."

Fine. I tell her everything that's gone on since the last time we spoke.

"So," Pearl says when I'm done, "will he take a kitten?"

"That's all you have to say about the lunch?"

"What else is there to say?" she asks. "My opinion hasn't changed. You *will* sleep with him. All of this is just prolonged foreplay. Save me time on phone calls and do it already."

My phone dings with a text from Blue.

You'd also save ME time listening in on your inane conversations.

I swear, sometimes I wish I'd been born a singleton. "Yeah, sure. I'll take one for the team. Did you have a position and location in mind?"

Pearl hums in exaggerated thought. "Position—reverse cowgirl? Location—and here I assume you don't mean pussy vs. butt—if it weren't so far away, I'd suggest The Palace Hotel. You know, where the wedding will be."

I nearly choke on my burrito. "What wedding?"

"You didn't get it?" Pearl asks.

"Get what?"

Blue chimes in via a text message:

The thing is very gaudy.

I glare at my screen. "What are you talking about?"

"Have you checked your mail?" Pearl asks.

I shake my head before I realize Pearl can't see me (but Blue probably can). "I'll do it now."

I take a big bite of my dinner and then go get the mail, which I riffle through, looking for something gaudy. Boy, do I find the *it*. A thing that is to other envelopes what Liberace was to the rest of the human race.

"Are these real jewels?" I ask into the phone as I open the ostentatious concoction.

"Probably," Pearl says. "And before you ask, yes, you *are* allowed to pawn this."

That wasn't what I was going to ask, but that's a great idea.

I pull the letter out—and gasp. The letter isn't

paper. It's gold made into a thin sheet, with words engraved on it:

You and a Plus One are cordially invited to the wedding of Miss Gia Hyman and His Royal Highness, Anatolio Cezaroff.

And so on and so forth.

Unbelievable. Until today, I thought the best magic trick of Gia's career was dating a real-life prince, but now she's actually marrying him. In the very hotel where she does her magic show.

"Is she going to be called a princess once it's a done deal?" I ask, eyes still on the invite.

"Not sure," Pearl says. "But if so, she'll force us to call her exclusively Princess Gia."

In Gia's defense, so would I.

"So unfair," Pearl mutters. "Marrying a prince was *my* dream, not hers. All she ever wanted was to be a female David Blaine. Or Copperfield. Or Goliath."

"Goliath wasn't a David; he was killed by one."

"It's called a joke," Pearl says snidely. "Also, Goliath was a giant—which matches Gia's magician persona's ego."

I finally tear my gaze away from the ludicrous invite. "Are you bringing a Plus One?"

"Nope, it's a paid gig for me. I was told there would be rich cheese connoisseurs there, so I begged Gia to let me cater the hors d'oeuvres."

I grin. "All cheese-related, no doubt."

"It's an opportunity of a lifetime."

"What about the rest of our clutch?" I ask.

Blue replies instantly, *I'm bringing Max. You should take Gunther.*

"Olive will bring her Florida man," Pearl says. "Lemon will obviously be with her new dancing husband. Holly will have her video game dude along and Blue her spy squeeze. I haven't spoken to Pixie for a few days, but I bet—"

"Will our parents be there?" I ask worriedly.

"No, they'll miss their firstborn's wedding."

A text from Blue chimes in:

Is Gia the firstborn, or is it Holly?

I ignore my sisters as the enormity of the situation hits me.

If I'm the only single sister out of eight, the full might of Mom's unholy attention will be on me—and she's already been worried about my dating prospects on account of my piercings and tattoos, even if she doesn't admit it.

Shit. If I don't bring someone, Mom might take it into her head to "have a talk" with me—and I don't want to hear about the benefits of orgasms for the millionth time.

I pinch the bridge of my nose, trying to think of what to do. My disastrous so-called love life doesn't help matters, especially my last clusterfuck of a relationship. I thought Spike was it for me. I had his name tattooed on my body, and—much more committing—I told my parents about him being "the one." Life and men being what they are, two months later, I had to tell my parents that he and I "consciously uncoupled" (his words, not mine) and I turned his name into a tattoo of a unicorn-shaped piñata with a hoop piercing in his well-endowed horse-like shlong. Just to clarify, the well-endowed part refers to the unicorn, not to Spike. The latter was average at best.

"You'd better reply soon," Pearl says, dragging me out of my gloomy contemplations. "You know how Gia gets."

I do and I don't. When we were children, Gia's displeasure could mean pepper in panties or toothpaste instead of frosting on a cupcake. But what can she do nowadays? On second thought, it's so much easier to just RSVP promptly for her wedding and not find out.

"Let me go do that," I say. "Talk tomorrow."

Fourteen

As I work out with Gunther the next day, I can't help the giddy feeling from knowing that we're going to lunch after this. I suppress it as much as I can, but it bubbles up like the fizz in a shaken bottle of soda. I do my best not to think about what it all means and keep a casual demeanor. Once in the cafeteria, we order and chat about work for a bit, and then I remember that he never told me if he'll take the kitten.

"You still owe me an answer," I say as the waiter comes with our food—Gunther's order from yesterday but this time for the both of us.

Gunther raises an eyebrow.

I wait for the waiter to leave before I clarify, "The tempting proposition I made to you."

The eyebrow is joined by a light wrinkle of his forehead.

"You know," I say. "The one regarding a pussy… cat."

Judging by how loudly he clears his throat, my words have nearly made him choke. "You're talking about the incestual kitten?"

With a smirk, I nod and sample the Eggs Benedict—and moan in pleasure.

He looks like he's still choking. "I have a few concerns regarding the *kitten*."

"Like?" I contemplate which knife to use to cut my eggs, then decide on breaking them with a fork, to avoid another lecture about table manners.

He frowns at what I've done with my fork, so I guess I've goofed anyway. But instead of a lecture, he asks, "Can cats get stung by bees?"

"Yeah," I say, remembering an incident on my parents' farm. "When I saw it happen, the kitty's reaction was mild—but my parents took it to the vet anyway because a small minority of cats can be allergic, just like people."

He scratches his chin. "What's the chance that the kitten you give me is one of those rare cases? I have more bees around than most people."

"The chance is low, but they do make EpiPens for cats just in case. Do you keep bees indoors? Or would you plan to let your cat roam outside?"

"No indoor bees," he says definitively. "But yeah, I believe it might be nice for a cat to be able to go outside."

Hmm. Would my feline homicidal maniac like to live outside part of the time? No. Not practical in

Manhattan—but maybe more doable in the part of Jersey where you can keep beehives.

I sample the avocado toast and find it much too delicious for something so simple. "On the off chance your cat turns out to be allergic, you could set up a screened catio outside."

He nods. "I might add one for me too. An actual patio, I mean. At the moment, I can't eat watermelon outside on a hot day—I get too much unwanted attention."

I picture watermelon juices flowing down his naked chest and sympathize with the bees. "There you go. Everyone wins."

For the rest of the meal, we discuss our likes and dislikes outside of music and movies. When the offer of dessert comes, I get ice cream again, and this time, my sundae is even fancier—because I came prepared with extra ingredients.

"What do you think?" I ask when I'm done.

"I think that's more of a banana split now," Gunther says. "And I think that carrying a banana in your pocket to save a few bucks is overkill."

"It was a means to an end." But the mention of bananas in pockets reminds me… When we hugged the other day, I could've sworn I felt—

"Speaking of means to ends," he says. "The company party this Friday is a way of building stronger team bonds. As a new team member, you could use that the most, so I want to make sure you're going."

I blink at him. "There's a company party?"

Is that a curse he just muttered under his breath? "You were supposed to be invited. Everyone was."

"Oh? By whom?"

"Tiffany."

That bitch. "Seems like inviting *me* slipped her mind."

"I'm sorry about that," he says earnestly. "Consider this your official invitation."

Oh, shit. Why didn't I just keep my mouth shut? The sweat I diligently washed away at the gym creeps back, and my overworked muscles tense. It's bad enough I have to worry about going to a royal wedding without a Plus One; now I have to deal with this company party crap. I've got nothing to wear. I have no idea how to—

"You look like I'm asking you to sleep on a bed of nails," he says.

All my dirty mind hears is "sleep," "bed," and something about getting nailed. "Why should I go where I'm not wanted?"

He frowns. "I'm sure Tiffany simply forgot to invite you."

"Yeah. Right. She's a saint, that one."

"Well, invitation aside, I think you should be there," he says. "And if you weren't going to come, I'd want it to be for the right reasons—and I can't think of any."

I grunt in frustration. "How would you like it if I insisted you come with me to some rando event out of the blue?"

He smirks. "I'd say, 'Thank you for thinking of me.'"

"Oh, yeah? In that case, you are formally invited as my Plus One to my sister's big, fancy wedding."

There. I think a part of me really wanted to invite him, but now that the words are out, I want to shove them back into my stupid mouth. The problems with him going would be incalculable. He'd meet the crazy bunch that is my family. Said family would believe I'm going to marry him—the man who ruined my life. And that's just the start.

Wait. I'm worried over nothing. There's no way he'd agree to my crazy proposition. He's not—

"Yes," he says, startling me.

"Huh?"

His smirk turns cocky. "Yes, I'll go to your thing if you go to mine."

Oh, boy. "'My thing' is a royal wedding."

His eyebrow arcs into a sideways question mark. "Royal?"

"Yeah." I tell him about how my sister Gia met her daredevil prince, concluding with, "So just imagine how stiff and proper you'd have to act at this shindig."

He shrugs. "That only makes me want to go more, not less. I'm not you."

Fuck. I forgot that stiff and proper are his middle names.

"I have nothing to wear to either event," I mutter.

My usual modus operandi is to buy a dress for some outing and then return it—but that's gotten me blacklisted from too many stores to count.

A glint enters his eyes. "What if *I* buy you a dress?"

That's evil. "Are you trying to tempt me with a freebie?"

"Is it working?"

I shake my head, but it's a weak shake and I think he can tell.

"Did I say *a* dress?" he asks guilelessly. "I meant *dresses*, one for each of the outings, of course."

Evil doesn't even cut it. A dress suitable for Gia's wedding is bound to cost a fortune—not to mention the torture of locating a store I'd be welcome in, trying stuff on, keeping it clean, and then returning it after.

"If I say yes, will you get the dresses without me— and send them to my house?" I look down at my getup. "You know, the way you did with the dorky work clothes?"

He appreciatively looks over the clothes he purchased for me. "Yes, though the stuff you have on is *not* dorky."

My deal mode is fully activated. "What about the wedding present?"

He narrows his eyes. "You want *me* on the hook for a gift for *your* sister's wedding?"

"Touché." I eat the last of my ice cream. "I guess with the job you've given me, I *can* afford it."

And maybe there's going to be some slick deal on something between now and then.

"It's settled then." He mimes at the waiter for the check, and when we get it, Gunther throws a wad of cash onto it—an exuberant tip, if anyone were to ask me, especially considering Gunther owns the place.

"Want to head up to our floor?" I ask as the memory of yesterday's hug resurfaces with the power of all my hormones.

His eyes shine a brighter green. "Let's go."

Fifteen

WE TAKE THE ELEVATOR UP IN A PECULIARLY TENSE silence. I don't know about Gunther, but our goodbye hug is all I can think about. However, when we get to his office, he cowardly slinks inside—no mention of a hug, not even a "see you later."

I swallow my disappointment. His actions make sense. The coworkers around us might not consider a hug appropriate, not to mention the high premiums Gunther would have to pay for building insurance if Tiffany's brain exploded all over the walls from jealousy.

For the rest of the day, I work in a haze. When I get home, three packages are waiting for me—one labeled Louis Vuitton, one Christian Dior, and the third Manolo Blahnik.

As my cat watches with slitted eyes, I rip into the boxes like a woman possessed by rabid wolverines. In a matter of moments, I get the contents out.

There are two cocktail dresses, one black, one red, and a pair of gold heels that would go with both. I gulp, examining the dresses. Each would show *a lot* of skin, especially the red one.

I guess Gunther is not bothered by the idea of my tattoos in a festive setting.

Knowing that Pearl would never forgive me if I didn't loop her in, I put on the black dress and videocall the little gossip.

"Wow," she says. "He wants you even more than I thought."

"Yeah. Sure." I change into the red dress, and my sister wolf-whistles when I let her see the result.

"Wear red to the wedding," she orders. "If he doesn't ravish you after seeing that, I'll up the promised year's supply of cheese to a decade's worth."

"That's a cheesy commitment."

She squints into the camera. "You'll be the hottest person at the event—with our face, anyway. I'm glad I'll be wearing a server's uniform and therefore not competing."

I smirk. "It's a good thing Gia and I don't share an identical face. She'd be pissed if I got to be the hottest at her wedding."

Pearl grins. "She'd only be pissed if you wore a white dress."

As we chat some more, I prepare myself some dinner, snap a picture of it, and send it to Gunther—all without telling Pearl a word about it because she'd think we have some weird BDSM setup going on, or something equally ridiculous.

"I've got to go," Pearl says. "Atonic's pregnancy is making her extra cranky, and she needs some attention right now."

"Tell her hi," I say and hang up.

Just then, the cause of said pregnancy saunters into the room, his expression grumpy.

Do you remember your purpose, It-that-feeds-me?

Yeah, yeah.

I set up a can of cat food for him before I dare to dig into my meal.

———

"Can I eat a piece of your steak?" Gunther asks after I order it for lunch the next day.

"I guess," I say. "But what about your iron?"

He displays the inside of his muscular, veiny arm. "I'm giving blood today, so I figure a bite is okay."

I'm glad I'm sitting because my knees go so violently wobbly I would've lost my footing for sure.

Gunther sits straighter. "Has your sugar dropped *again*?"

Fuck. He gave me some of his protein shake at the gym, so if I keep up with the low-blood-sugar narrative, he'll start feeding me more, and I'll get as big as an International House of Pancakes.

A strange temptation nibbles at me. For some reason, I feel like I can trust him with my secret. Maybe because he's opened up to me about his shameful Kenny G fetish.

"Hand me your phone," I demand.

Looking confused, he hands me the device.

I put my finger to my mouth in a "hush" gesture, then carry his phone and my phone to a table that's out of earshot of ours—in case Blue happens to be listening.

When I come back, Gunther is looking at me like I've lost my last marbles, so I whisper, "My sister Blue used to work for a certain government agency that likes to poke its nose into everyone's electronic business. Because of that, I don't trust secrets around devices."

Gunther's worried expression morphs into an intrigued one. "Secrets?"

"*A* secret. Singular." I take a breath. "It's not the blood sugar that made me blanch, but it *is* related to blood."

"Blood? Why? Is it that time of the month?"

He seems to be perfectly fine saying that, whereas I cringe at the pictures in my mind. We clearly have a role reversal going on, where it's the guy who mentions period blood without blinking an eye, and the girl who's grossed out.

"It's not that," I say when I recover. "I'm just not a fan of talking about blood. Or seeing it. Or thinking about it. Especially the idea of it being drawn." What I don't add is that I particularly don't like the idea of blood lost by people I care about, since I don't want him to think I consider him in that category.

Because I don't.

This is more of a generic reaction.

Yeah. I'm sticking to that.

His eyes go wide. "So that time when you fainted—"

"Ashildr's nose was dry and—"

"Say no more," Gunther says. "I don't want you to relive that incident and feel worse."

"Thanks."

"But why lie about your hemophobia?"

I wrinkle my nose. "It's not hemophobia."

He nods sagely. "Sorry to try and label, but you know what I mean. Why tell me it was your blood sugar level?"

"Isn't it obvious?" I peer into his eyes. "It's a weakness—so I never tell anyone about it."

He scoffs. "That's *not* a weakness."

"Agree to disagree."

"Well, would you feel better if I told you my fear is much weaker sounding than yours?"

"Maybe. Is it clowns?"

He opens his mouth, but the waiter comes with our food.

When the waiter leaves, Gunther reaches forward with his fork. "So, what say you about that piece of steak?"

I slap his hand away. "Nice try. Spill it."

He looks at the steak longingly, but then he shakes his head. "Not worth it."

"No. You have to tell me. You can't bring up something like that and not tell me. Besides, I told you mine."

"Fine." He extends his hand again, and I cut him a piece. I even use the proper hand for each utensil.

Once he finishes his treat, he furtively looks around and whispers, "Arachibutyrophobia."

I blink. "Spiders?"

"That's arachno-phobia. *Arachne* means spider in Greek."

"What does your fear mean in Greek?" I bet it's a phobia of having lunch companions with a diminished vocabulary.

He looks around again. "*Arachi* means 'ground nuts' and—"

"Ouch. So it's a fear of getting your testicles smashed? Doesn't every guy have that?"

He sighs. "I'm not finished. *Butyr* stands for 'butter,' so—"

"Nut butter?" Hopefully *not* the testicle kind—I'd be afraid of that too.

"Specifically, peanut butter," he says with distaste. "More specifically, it's a fear of having it stick to the roof of my mouth."

I narrow my eyes. "Didn't you tell me you were allergic?"

His muscular shoulders move up and down, like when he does the military press. "You're not the only one who knows how to lie to cover up their phobia."

I stare at him, words momentarily failing me.

"Some think it sounds silly, but at its core, it's a fear of suffocation," he says defensively.

I vehemently shake my head. "I don't think it's silly. I think it sucks."

"Thanks," he says. "My father told me I saw my cousin go into anaphylactic shock after eating peanut butter. My cousin's throat started to close up, and saving him required a trip to the ER—so it was all pretty scary, especially for a child. I don't remember any of this happening, but it does sound like a plausible explanation for why I developed that particular phobia."

I reach out and place my hand on his. "I'm sorry that happened to little you."

Looking uncomfortable, he gently pulls his hand away.

Fuck. Have I overstepped the employee/employer boundaries yet again?

"It's not a big deal," he says, but he doesn't sound convincing. "So many people are deathly allergic to peanuts nowadays that I rarely come across the stuff. I figure blood isn't as easy to avoid."

"Sadly, it's not."

He locks eyes with me. "Did you also have a catalyst for your situation, or was it just something that—"

"Yes," I say. "But if I tell you, it stays between us."

"Sure."

"No." I wave my knife. In case that seems too threatening, I put it down. "I really mean it. You're going to meet my family at the wedding, and I don't want them to know about the blood thing or the so-called catalyst."

He puts his hand on his chest. "If I ever spill your secret, may my mouth fill up with peanut butter."

I glance furtively in the direction of our phones, then whisper, "In my family, we call the event in question the Zombie Tit Massacre."

I wait for him to chuckle, but he looks horrified instead—which is the appropriate reaction—so I continue. "Remember that farm my parents own?"

He gives a barely noticeable nod, like he's afraid a more sudden movement might spook me.

"Well, my parents have all sorts of rescue animals there, and at some point, they gave shelter to one *parus major*—a bird more colloquially known as The Great Tit." Still not even a hint of a smile on his face, despite all the 'tit' references. Impressive. I go on, watching him closely. "What's more important is that this bird also goes by the Zombie Tit on account of its legit thirst for brains. In the wild, the brains they crave are those of bats, but as it turns out, on a farm, they'll attack chickens just as happily."

"Oh, no," he mutters.

"Oh, yes. My clutch mate Blue walked in on the whole thing and has been deathly afraid of birds ever since. My sister Gia—the royal bride at the wedding we're attending—was second on the scene, and she's a germaphobe to this day."

He looks confused, probably wondering why I hide my own experience if I have two sisters who can relate.

"Anyway," I continue. "After they ran home and told the rest of us what happened, I snuck out and did the dumbest thing I could've possibly done—I checked out the murder scene."

"Why?" he whispers.

I blow out a frustrated breath. "Not sure what I was thinking. I *was* obsessed with appearing tough back then, so maybe it was a test of my mettle." I shudder. "I only saw a brief glimpse of what happened to those chickens, but it was enough. I haven't been able to look at a drop of blood ever since." My smile is strained as I add, "Stupid, right?"

I don't think he realizes what he's doing when he covers my hand with his. "You weren't stupid. You were just curious. I probably would've done the same as a kid."

Must. Not. Sniffle. He already thinks I'm a ninny.

I take a deep breath, and when I have my emotions under control, I glance at his comforting hand with gratitude—which is, sadly, when he awkwardly pulls it away.

"How about we talk about something else?" I suggest, injecting cheer into my voice.

"Yeah, sure."

"Hold that thought," I say and go get our phones.

When I'm back, he asks, "Do you really think the government cares about what you told me?"

I cover my phone's mic and whisper, "Not the government, per se, more like a certain sister who worked for them and learned how to snoop."

146

"Oh. I see. I still can't believe she doesn't know about your thing."

"No one does. You're the first person I've ever told."

And if Blue is listening right now and dying of curiosity, serves her right.

His eyes gleam. "Thank you for trusting me."

Worried that a sniffle is not far away, I wave his nice words away. "What about you?" I ask nonchalantly. "I take it you don't keep yours a secret?"

His forehead wrinkles. "My parents know. And I told my ex—the one with whom things got pretty serious. But that's about it."

"You mean Tiffany?"

He looks at me like I'm crazy again. "Tiffany and I briefly dated in high school. It wasn't serious at all. I'd never have hired her otherwise."

"Huh."

He grins. "Also, don't forget: I was a teenage boy in high school, and they don't admit stuff like that."

"I repeat. Huh." Should I give myself permission to feel special? Maybe. First things first. "Who was that ex then?"

The grin dematerializes. "Her name was—*is*—Chelsey. She liked peanut butter a lot, so I had no choice but to fess up when we moved in together. Now, had I known she'd break off our engagement a year later, I would've lied and said I was allergic."

This time, I don't go for his hand, but the urge is there. "I'm sorry," I say softly.

He shrugs. "It's fine. She did me a favor. I'm not the marrying kind."

He's not? Not that I care, but isn't this something you tell a girl *before* you blackmail her to work for you, then ask her to work out with you and have lunches together and—

"What about you?" he asks. "Any serious relationships?"

Great. I have to tell him this shit now, too?

No choice, really.

Reluctantly, I share about Spike—but not everything, and especially not the tattoo part.

"That really sucks," Gunther says.

"Yeah," I say. "And that wasn't even the end of it. A week later, after I told him to die, he took my motorcycle on a joy ride and totaled it."

Gunther's eyes go slitty. "Did he at least break something?"

"Yeah. His hip—like an old lady."

"Good," Gunther surprises me by saying. "Serves the asshole right."

I flash him a grin. "Did you wish Chelsey would break her hip?"

He opens his mouth to answer, but the waiter comes back with an offer of dessert. Following tradition, I get ice cream, and when the waiter is gone, Gunther changes the topic to work matters— something I don't begrudge for a second.

After the meal, we walk together to the elevators,

quietly—me because I'm wondering if we'll hug goodbye or not, him a mystery.

In my defense, the last time he took the elevator down and I up, we totally hugged, so there is a precedent.

He stops.

I stop.

He presses the down button.

I press up.

He looks down at me with a strange expression.

Okay.

Fuck it.

I'm going to go for it.

Sixteen

I TAKE A STEP TOWARD GUNTHER.

He takes a step toward me.

Suddenly, I feel malevolent eyes piercing my back—and Gunther looks over my shoulder with a startled expression.

"Tiffany," he says before I can turn.

"Hello," she says in a voice so sweet her vocal cords must be on the verge of diabetes. "Fancy bumping into you."

An elevator opens—the one that's going up. "That's for you two," Gunther says and holds the door, ushering us in.

I don't know about Tiffany, but I feel like I'm walking the plank as I enter.

When the doors close, any pretense of friendliness leaves Tiffany's heavily made-up face.

"Are you still going to deny sleeping with the boss?" she demands.

I bare my teeth in a scathing smile. "Are you going to pretend you 'forgot' to invite me to the company party?"

She stands straighter. "Mr. Ferguson's retirement party? I obviously made a point not to invite you."

Wait. How can Gunther be retiring? He can't be.

Then it hits me. "You mean Mr. Ferguson senior?" I ask stupidly.

As in, Gunther's father?

She gives a derisive sniff. "You'd think a scammer would remember a man she defrauded. Then again, there must've been so many that it's hard for you to keep track."

I curse out loud, and not all of my words are aimed at Tiffany. Some of the choicest words express my feelings about going to Gunther's father's retirement party.

The elevator stops, the doors open, and I see Ashildr along with a few other co-workers—which makes me swallow the rest of my soliloquy.

Tiffany, being a coward, darts out of the car, but I don't give her chase. Instead, I walk slowly as I digest the retirement bombshell.

Gunther's father will obviously be at his own retirement party—which means I might bump into him. I don't want to face him. Tiffany might've been on to something when she didn't invite me.

But why does Gunther want me there? Doesn't he realize this problem?

The worst part is that I can't flake out. Not when

Gunther's already bought me a fancy dress, and his being my Plus One at the wedding is predicated on my attendance at the party.

Fuck.

When Gunther returns from let's-not-think-where-he-was, I contemplate walking into his office and raising the issue of my meeting with his father, but the Band-Aid in the crook of his elbow is a serious deterrent, so I chicken out and promise myself that I'll bring it up tomorrow.

It doesn't happen. Even though I have plenty of time while we exercise together and have lunch, I have trouble raising the topic. I do learn more about Gunther, however—like, for example, that he went to Michigan State University on a football scholarship and earned his Bachelor of Science in a major called Packaging, which has something to do with the consumer goods industry and nothing to do with his package.

The next day is the day of the party, so it's too late to back out. Instead, I come to work early so I can leave early, and when I get home, Pearl is already waiting for me there, her makeup kit in hand.

"This is going to be fun," she says with a big grin.

"Arguable," I reply before plopping in a chair in my living room and allowing her to do her worst to my face.

After what feels like an hour, she puts a mirror in front of me. "Don't you think you look gorge?"

"You gave me makeup like this for my Harley Quinn costume for Halloween back in high school."

She beams proudly. "You're welcome."

"It wasn't a compliment."

She dabs my cheek with one last touch of foundation. "Don't care. You look amazeballs. Especially in those shoes."

I glance at the high-heeled torture contraptions Gunther bought me and sigh. Then I check out the clock. Yep. If I don't want to be majorly late, this makeup and these shoes will have to suffice.

"Thanks," I say grudgingly. "I'd better go."

———

When the cab drops me off at the venue—Metropolitan Pavilion—I almost ask the driver to take me home.

But no. I've already come this far, might as well go all the way.

I clickety-click inside, my ass swaying unnaturally thanks to the Manolo Blahnik fuck-me pumps—or whatever they're called.

The security lets me in—damn Gunther—and much too soon, I step into the twenty-five-thousand-square-foot ballroom space filled with drinking, munching, and crunching Munch & Crunch employees.

The music—if you can call it that—sounds like the angry cries of a baby birthed by elevator muzak, after she'd been fucked by an ice cream truck jingle... with a penis shaped like a saxophone.

On a hunch, I use my phone to identify the artist responsible.

Yep. Kenny G. Or what he sounds like when remixed by a DJ.

If this atrocity is playing, Gunther shouldn't be far.

I look up from my phone and realize I might be a little psychic because there he is.

And fuck. In theory, he looks the same. Same slicked-back dark hair, same nice suit—but something is different. Better. Maybe he got a haircut? Or this is his best-fitting suit?

The bottom line is, I want to lick his chiseled face, starting with his sexy lips.

"Hi," he says gruffly, his eyes roaming over my body —no doubt cataloging (and disapproving of) the tattoos he hasn't seen before.

"Want to take a picture?" I ask pointedly.

He seems to snap out of the tattoo-trance or whatever it was. "You look stunning."

I roll my eyes. "Is that a compliment for me, or for your dress-choosing skills?"

With a grin, he grabs two champagne flutes from a passing waiter and hands one to me. "I have a feeling you like free drinks."

Like? Love is more apropos.

"Thanks." As I grab the flute, my fingers brush his— and I already feel intoxicated. Nodding at the giant stockpile of alcohol in the distance, I ask, "Is that an open bar as well?"

"Of course. It's a party."

Now would be a good time to ask if I could dodge his father, who seems to be the main reason for the event. Just as I open my mouth to do that, Gunther says, "Come, there's someone I want you to speak with."

He strides purposefully into the crowd, and I follow like a sheep. We stop a few feet away from the mega-bar, next to a familiar gray-haired gentleman wearing a Hawaiian shirt.

Oh, no. Is this—

"Dad," Gunther says, confirming my suspicions. "This is Ms. Hyman."

Seventeen

I DOWN MY CHAMPAGNE IN ONE GULP. HERE WE GO. "Honey, please."

"What a cute endearment for your boss," Gunther's father says, eyes crinkling. "If I hadn't retired today, I would've insisted everyone at the office call *me* 'honey' going forward."

Gunther grunts. "Come on, Dad. You know she didn't call me that."

Gunther's dad looks at me guilelessly. "You didn't?"

"Nope. Honey is *my* name," I say. "So please call me that."

Maybe this won't be as awful as I feared.

Gunther's dad extends his hand. "In that case, call me Gunther."

"Oh?" I turn to my Gunther... I mean, the younger Gunther. "All this time you've hidden the fact that you're a Junior."

Gunther Senior covers his mouth theatrically.

"Sorry, son. Now you'll end up going by G.J. at the office, the way you did at home."

"Not necessarily," I deadpan. "At the office, we already call him Mr. Snookums."

His dad chuckles as Gunther grumbles, "Mr. Snookums sounds like a cat."

"What sounds like a cat?" Ashildr asks, appearing out of the crowd.

Shit. Is this place humid enough? The last thing I want is for Ashildr's nose to feel too dry and commit seppuku. If I swoon in front of Senior, I'll never live it down. Worse yet, he'll think I'm on drugs.

"Mr. Snookums is my alleged nickname at the office," Gunther says.

Ashildr pales—which is good in that the blood has just rushed far away from his nose. "Sir," he says solemnly. "I've never heard that said about you. If I do, I will put a swift stop to it."

Senior leans down and into my ear says, "Ashildr is one of the good ones."

"Thank you, sir," Ashildr says, looking on the verge of tearing up. "And congratulations. Again."

Senior raises his glass and drains the little bit of the rich amber liquid that remains at the bottom. He must've had the rest of it earlier—which may explain his jovial mood.

"If I could borrow you for a second…" Ashildr says to the younger Gunther.

"It should be: 'May I borrow you for a second… Mr. Snookums,'" I say.

Gunther levels an emerald-eyed glare at me before letting Ashildr lead him away.

Crap. Now I'm on my own with the very man I meant to hide from. My luck never disappoints.

As if to confirm my fears, Senior's expression turns more serious. "Gunther has been telling me about your progress."

"He has?" Has he told him about the pranks? The hug? The fainting?

Senior nods. "He tells me the work you're doing is phenomenal."

I nearly drop my empty flute. "This is the first I'm hearing of it."

Senior sighs. "If there's one thing Gunther could still learn about management, it's how to deliver praise when it's due."

I strive to recover my composure. "I guess with you retiring, Gunther will have to tell me personally how phenomenal my work is."

The laugh lines in the corners of Senior's eyes crinkle. "That's why I had to retire. Maybe now my son will step up and deliver a basic compliment on his own."

I clear my throat. Here goes nothing. "Sir. About high school... I wanted to—"

"Stop right there," Senior says. "I don't hold any grudges. If anything, your redemption story warms my heart." He smiles at me full-on, making it apparent where Gunther got his sexy grin from. "I'm just glad I

158

listened to him back then, when he suggested I drop any charges and ask the principal to go easy on you."

I take a step back. "By 'him,' do you mean Gunther?"

"Who else?"

I blink uncomprehendingly. "Why would Gunther tattletale on me if he didn't want you to get me in trouble?"

Senior looks at me like I'm as stupid as I feel. "Gunther wasn't the one who told me."

"No? Then who?"

Senior darts a quick glance at the crowd, then back at me. "Even though it's been a while, I don't think I feel comfortable betraying something said in confidence. I hope you understand."

I sneak a peek at where I think he looked.

Of course.

Tiffany.

I should've known.

My heart picks up pace.

All this time, I thought it was Gunther who'd ruined my life, but it had always been her. First by ratting on me to Gunther Senior, then by being there for my knife to penetrate her skin.

Okay, maybe the knife thing was a little more on me.

Fine, maybe more than a little.

"There you are," an attractive older woman says to Senior after flashing a dimpled smile.

"Hey, honey," Senior says to her. Turning to me, he

says, "I meant my wife this time. Sorry if that was confusing."

"Ah, so you're Honey." The newcomer extends her hand to me. "I'm Jennifer. Gunther's mom. *Your* Gunther."

Mine? I shake her hand and say that it's nice to meet her.

She hugs Senior possessively. "Was *my* Gunther keeping you entertained?"

Before I can answer, Tiffany strides over. My hackles rise—and until this moment I was pretty confident that only dogs had hackles.

"Evening, Jen," Tiffany says in her most treacle tone. "Congrats, Mr. Ferguson."

Is it sexist that "Jen" isn't "Mrs. Ferguson"? Also, how inappropriate would it be if I started choking Tiffany in front of everyone? I don't mean to suffocate her, just until—

"Why don't we let them chat?" says Gunther's mom, a.k.a. Jennifer to most people, a.k.a. Jen to rude bitches. "Tiffany no doubt has a lot of nice words to say to the man who got her her current job."

Oh. So Senior asked Gunther to hire her? I don't know why, but I like that it wasn't my Gunther's idea.

I let Jennifer pull me away to the less busy part of the bar, and we both order fresh drinks—a Cosmo for her and a Long Island iced tea for me.

Dragging me farther out of earshot of Senior and Tiffany, she whispers, "My husband is wonderful, but he has one flaw. He is much too friendly with young women who cross his path, even if they're his son's ex-girlfriends. Just so you know, *that* is the only reason *she's* here." She gestures at a beautiful woman in the crowd.

I blink and examine the woman in question more closely. Blond and blue-eyed, she has a snooty pout to her lips and lots of filler at random places on her face. When the stranger spots Jennifer looking at her, she waves and smiles a centerfold's smile.

"Who is it?" I ask.

"Chelsey," Jennifer says with distaste. "Even after she broke up with my son, my husband let her keep her job at one of the franchises. And now she's here too."

Chelsey? She of the broken engagement? What was Senior thinking?

All of a sudden, I'm not sure whom I'd choose if I were allowed to choke only one person tonight.

"Sorry," Jennifer says. "Chelsey is beyond irrelevant now, and definitely not worth any attention."

"Agreed," I say firmly.

Jennifer's smile is contagious as she says, "I hear you and Gunther have been working out together."

"Junior only," I say.

She grabs my elbow. "And there have been daily lunches."

I smile. "Gunther tells you a lot, doesn't he?"

"He's a good boy." She lets my elbow go and whispers into my ear, "What I wanted to tell you was—make sure you fill out the 66669 HR form."

Why does that sound familiar? Oh, yeah. 666 and 69. That's the HR form for dating.

Wait…

"We're not dating," I blurt.

"Who says you are?" She winks at me. "But if you were, make sure not to get into trouble. Either of you. I speak from personal experience, since I also met my husband at work, and things almost went south when—"

"That story again?" Gunther Junior says, appearing out of the crowd. Turning to me, he adds, "Mom likes to tell everyone who'll listen how she and Dad met."

"When you get to my age, you'll also be bugging people with tales of how you met your wife." For whatever reason, Jennifer looks meaningfully at me before stating, "Since it's my time, I'll tell the story."

And she does. Apparently, she and her husband were a cliché—he the boss and she the secretary. Then, at a company party, they got drunk and gropey in front of everyone. Since Senior was the boss, some asshole from HR tried to fire Jennifer for "unseemly behavior," but in the end, Senior fired the asshole instead and married her.

"And I'd marry you again," Senior says as he and Tiffany rejoin us. With a bow, he extends his hand to his wife. "Want to dance?"

Blushing, Jennifer lets him lead her away, leaving me in the company of Gunther and Tiffany.

"Isn't this your favorite song?" Tiffany asks as a

slow rock ballad begins. Looking at me, she adds in a superior tone, "It's *Don't Speak* by No Doubt."

"Then it can't be his favorite," I say. "That honor belongs to something awful by Kenny G."

Gunther opens his mouth to weigh in, but his breath catches as he stares at something behind me.

I turn.

Fuck.

It's Chelsey, sauntering our way.

Is this my punishment for dissing *Scott Pilgrim vs. the World*? Is the universe making *me* confront a bunch of evil exes?

"Hi," she says seductively, her eyes on Gunther and the rest of her pretending that Tiffany and I do not exist.

"What are you doing here?" Gunther asks coldly.

"It's our song," Chelsey says, waving at a nearby speaker. "I thought maybe we could dance. For old times' sake."

I'm pretty sure the expression on Gunther's face is the same one he'd have if peanut butter got stuck to the roof of his mouth. "As you know, I only dance with my dates." To my utter shock, he grabs my hand. "Honey, would you like to dance to my favorite non-Kenny-G song?"

"With pleasure," I reply. Because what else can I say?

"Honey is her name," Tiffany butts in. "Not an endearment."

Chelsey finally deigns to acknowledge my existence. "*This* is your date?"

"Watch out," Tiffany says. "She can cut you." It seems like she wants to say more, but a glare from Gunther shuts her up beautifully.

Should I explain how choking would be my modus operandi tonight instead of cutting?

Nah.

Grabbing Gunther by the elbow, I smile evilly at his two exes and drag him onto the dance floor.

"Thank you," he says with feeling. "I owe you one."

"In that case, as payment, I'd like you to help me make this dance business look good."

He frowns. "You don't know how to dance?"

"I can skank."

He glances back at Chelsey, or maybe Tiffany. "That's too harsh."

I snort. "I wasn't calling anyone here a skank. Skank is the name of the dance you do to punk music." I stand with my weight slightly forward, then raise a leg off the ground, bend it, and kick forward—almost into Gunther's shin. To fully illustrate the skank, I hop onto the leg that just kicked and swing my arms—nearly punching out a few nearby employees as I go.

Gunther beams at me. "How about we dance like everyone else?" He gestures around.

Hmm.

Everyone else is standing close together, ballroom style.

What was I thinking when I dragged him here?

"You can do it," he says reassuringly.

Or I can make a fool of myself in front of his parents and exes. "Can you lead?"

He stands in a gentlemanly posture with hands outstretched. I put my hands into his—and hold my breath.

With a cocky grin, he pulls me close. And I mean way, way too close. Close enough to smell the beeswax and smoke on his skin, mixed with something deliciously male. Close enough to feel how hard his leg muscles are as they touch mine.

"Now we sway," he whispers right into my ear and matches actions to words.

Holy Sex Pistols.

Have I had too much to drink, or is this just my normal reaction to his proximity?

My nipples are as hard as if they'd smashed into an ice sculpture, my panties are begging for a dryer, and my brain is a hormone smoothie.

"That's it," he murmurs. "You're doing good."

Am I? I'm not stepping on his feet, so that's something. Nor am I copping a feel of Mr. Suck & Lick, even though I can feel that particular creature hulking out of Gunther's pants—no doubt due to some unfathomable quirk of the friction created by our dancing.

Gunther must realize I've noticed his arousal. He puts a little distance between us—a move that paradoxically makes me want to jump him all the more.

"The song is almost over," he whispers, his lips

brushing my earlobe in a gentle caress that would make me come on the spot if my ear pulled a *Freaky Friday* and swapped places with my clit.

"So what do we do now?" I ask breathlessly.

"Drinks?" he suggests. "Ideally, away from everyone."

"Sure." I sneak a glance at "everyone." Tiffany and Chelsey seem to be bickering about something, both looking like they might pull each other's hair—or uterus—out at any second.

Gunther disengages from the dance pose with a bow, then follows my gaze with a frown. "Can I ask for a favor?"

"Yes?" *Please let it be a sexual one.*

"Once we get those drinks, maybe you could look like you're having fun?"

Huh. That shouldn't be hard. I always have fun when we're together, so extra alcohol should only enhance that. For obvious reasons, my reply is, "I'll do my best. It will have to be the performance of my life."

"I'm sure it will be a Herculean effort." Gunther summons the bartender and demands a whiskey neat for himself and another Long Island iced tea for me.

"Cheers." I clink against his glass and sip my drink. It tastes amazing, which means the bartender went light on the gin, rum, or vodka.

From a distance, I hear Chelsey's voice, but the only word I make out is "bitch." Or was it "witch?" Maybe "snitch?"

"We should probably get your parents out of their

vicinity," I say to Gunther. "Claws are about to come out, and we wouldn't want them to become collateral damage."

He gestures at the dance floor to our left. "I think they're a step ahead of you."

Yep. Jennifer and Senior are doing the Macarena—at least I think that's what the noise coming out of the speakers is called.

"Did Kenny G write this awfulness too?" I ask.

"This song is by Los del Río, and my dad is a big fan."

An echo of Tiffany's voice reaches my ears this time, and it sounds like "whore," though it's possible she said "bore" or "eyesore."

"We should play a drinking game," I tell Gunther. "Whenever those two say or do something catty, we take a drink."

He grins. "You're on."

Just in time, Chelsey calls Tiffany something that sounds like "blunt," or "grunt," or—and this might be my deal obsession warping my hearing—"discount."

We drink.

Tiffany calls Chelsey a slut, or possibly glut or nut.

Grinning, I drink, and Gunther follows.

Chelsey retorts by calling her opponent either a cow or a sow.

Gunther orders us another round of drinks, and we take our obligatory gulps in honor of the bovine (or possibly swine) insult.

Her voice getting louder, Tiffany says something

about Chelsey's mother or calls her a monster, so we drink again.

The battle goes on for a bit, and so does our drinking. That is, until Tiffany finds the right button to push—because Chelsey throws her drink into her face and storms off.

"I never thought I'd be grateful to Tiffany," I mutter, chugging down another drink as per the game. "I'm glad Chelsey is out of here."

Gunther just drinks, but the relieved expression on his face is unmistakable. He's either glad his former fiancée is gone, or that the drinking game is over.

On Tiffany's end, she looks around indignantly and slinks away, presumably to deal with her wet clothing —making this one of my favorite two-for-one deals.

"Want to dance again?" Gunther asks, his words slightly slurred.

Hmm. Another slow song is playing, so it's tempting. "We don't have to pretend to have fun anymore," I say regardless.

"I'm not pretending," he says. "Are you?

I shake my head.

"In that case…" He extends his hand gallantly. "The dance floor awaits."

I accept his hand, and the zing of his touch makes my head spin… so much so I lose my step for a second. The slow song ends, and another one starts. It has a fast beat and sounds very corporate—at least insofar as someone is chanting something about some clerk.

"Is this also Kenny G?" I ask Gunther.

"No," he says with a slight eyeroll. "This song has my dad written all over it. He's into songs that are named after a dance. I believe this one is called 'Twerk.'"

Huh. I guess it's not a clerk that they're chanting about. Oh, and this also explains the copious booty shaking happening on the dance floor.

"How much do you want to bet the next song is going to be 'Gangnam Style?'" Gunther shouts. "That or 'La Bamba.'"

"I want to try it," I shout back over a hiccup.

His nostrils flare. "Which of those three?"

"Just turn around."

He looks uncertain.

"Prude," I mutter and turn my back to him.

Okay. I've seen Miley Cyrus do this. I squat low and shake my butt.

Damn. This is harder than I thought, but I have a strategy: I focus on moving the tattoos on each of my butt cheeks up and down. The tattoos in question happen to be very realistically rendered nipples, so combined with what I'm currently doing, I feel like a burlesque performer—which might be what inspires me to thrust my booty backward, right into Gunther's crotch.

Was that a grunt of pain or pleasure? I turn to check, but it's unclear. All I know is that his mouth looks ridiculously sexy.

"Thanks," he says with a dose of masculine pride.

Wait. "Did I blurt that sexy mouth thing out loud?"

His cocky grin is my answer, and if I thought his mouth looked sexy before, it's irresistible now.

I stop the twerking and twirl—or pirouette, if we're talking dance moves.

Hmm. The twirl was probably too sudden. The room is now blurring around the edges, and I have a hard time standing straight.

"Here." Gunther puts a supporting hand on the small of my back and leans down. "Want to take a closer look at my mouth?"

I laugh—a bit too loudly if turning heads are anything to go by.

He licks his lips temptingly.

Fine. I grab a handful of his fancy tie and pull him all the way down.

Our lips clash. He tastes like caramel, oak, and charcoal with a hint of alcohol—probably all from the whiskey.

Did I call his mouth sexy? I should've been more generous. It's delicious. Wonderful. Sublime.

The room spins around us, and everything but the kiss seems to disappear.

He grabs my butt cheeks, his thumbs near where the images of nipples are etched into my skin.

Fuck.

I feel as though my actual nipples are being stimulated—probably because they're so hard and pressed so tightly against the miles of stupid fabric separating our bodies.

Pulling away with extreme reluctance, I gasp, "We have to get out of here."

He grabs my hand and pulls me through our gyrating co-workers.

As we go, people must bump into us a lot because we're swaying from side to side, like pendulums in a hurricane.

Outside, a flotilla of black cars is waiting, so we jump into a random one.

"My place," I order.

The driver smiles. "And that would be?"

To my surprise, Gunther rattles out the address.

How did he—

Never mind. He shipped me the clothes I have on. The clothes that chafe, now that I think about it.

"Your mouth is sexy too," Gunther says, his voice low and husky. And maybe slightly slurred.

Replying doesn't seem like the best use of my tongue, so I let it wrestle with his instead.

By Ramones' balls, the only wrestling move I know is the stunner, and that's what it feels like Gunther is doing to my tongue.

Yum.

We wrestle like that some more, him stopping in wonder whenever he encounters the stud in my tongue, me melting into a puddle of oxytocin-flavored goo when he plays with it.

Time seems to slow. Or speed up. It gets fuzzy, that's for sure.

At some point, there's some major lip nibbling that I

can't force into the wrestling metaphor. Later still, his strong hand traces my jawline, his large fingers making me feel as dainty as a fairy princess.

And then the stupid car stops.

What the fuck? We're here already? And where are we?

I reluctantly unpeel my lips from Gunther's and check the view out the window.

Ah. Right. That's my building.

Gunther's eyes look molten as they peer into mine. "Now what?"

I want him to come up, but some part of me recalls that you don't just say, "Come fuck me, hard." You've got to be a little more subtle. I think. The problem is, I have trouble coming up with an alternative.

And then it hits me. "Come meet the father of your future baby."

Gunther exits the car without further urging, but the car driver checks the rearview mirror with a raised eyebrow. I guess there's kink, and then there's the male impregnating another male scenario I just accidentally implied.

"I mean his fur baby," I grumble as Gunther opens the door for me.

The driver doesn't seem to buy it, or maybe he doesn't believe that the explanation makes anything sound better.

After a hiccup, Gunther states, "I think I knew that's what you meant."

"Bunny," I clarify just in case.

"Don't you have a cat?" Gunther extends his hand to me. "You definitely mentioned a kitten… unless that's what they call a baby bunny as well?"

No. Maybe. A kid can be a baby goat, I know that much. But what do they call a baby bunny?

No idea, and I'm too horny to make my brain work that hard.

"Bunny is the cat's name," I say and use the proffered hand to get to my feet.

For some reason, the street goes loopy around me.

The car leaves with screeching tires, and I lean on Gunther, who sways a bit as a result.

"If you can call your cat Bunny, then I have a great name for the kitten," he says.

We take several steps toward the building before I ask, "Is that name a secret?"

"Ah," he says. "I thought I already said it."

"Nope."

"Bee," he says with great pride.

I process what he's said—which takes so long we're in the elevator by the time I ask, "For boy cat or a girl?"

His reply is on a delay too. "Either way," he says as I open my front door. "If it's a boy, it will be short for Beeowulf. Otherwise, Beeatrix."

"I doubt you ever won a spelling *bee* as a kid." I gesture for him to come inside.

As soon as he does, Bunny comes out and rubs himself against his leg—something he's never done in all of his nine lives.

"Baby daddy?" Gunther asks, peering at him.

I nod sadly. My sorry excuse for an excuse has just evaporated. "I know what you're thinking. Some cats look like they've eaten a canary, but this one looks like he he's waterboarded the poor bird first, plucked all its feathers, deprived it of sleep for a year, and then made it listen to some so-called music by Kenny G."

Gunther ignores the insult. Still looking at the cat, he asks, "Is his bed in your bedroom?"

"No," I blurt. "I mean... yes. Want to see?"

He nods.

Yes! I lead Gunther to the bedroom and close the door before Bunny can follow us. The last thing I want is for the cat to explain that his bed is actually perched on a tall shelf in the living room.

Gunther looks dizzy as he takes in the walls—probably because he's never seen so many posters for cool bands in one place.

I lay my hand on Gunther's buff shoulder to get his attention, and then my mouth spurts, "Your mouth doesn't just look sexy. It kisses sexy too."

Huh. Who knew *that* was the trigger phrase that Gunther was waiting for all this time? There's a hunger in his eyes when he turns to me, and before I can react, he captures my mouth with his.

Fuck. Why is time acting so weird? One moment, I'm in the middle of the most scorching kiss of my life; the next, Gunther is sliding my dress down—and my fingers are unzipping his pants.

We rip at the rest of our clothes as if getting the other person naked were a contest—which Gunther quickly wins. I'm completely exposed while he still has his boxers on, and he pulls out of my reach before I can rid him of them.

The reason he's stepped away quickly becomes clear. He wants to get a good look at me.

"Wow," he mutters after the examination is over.

Now that could be either a good wow or a bad one —all depends on how he feels about my assortment of piercings and tattoos. Oh, and my body, of course.

I step close to him, determined to claim those boxers. But first, I can't help but trace my fingers over the grooves on his naked chest. "Those workouts do your body good."

He waves my statement off, grabs my hand, and twirls me, explaining, "I want to see you from the back."

Does that mean that wow was a good wow? I mean, why see more of something that repulses you, right?

"Like a work of art," he says, twirling me back to face him.

"Like?" I ask indignantly.

"Sorry." He cradles my face in his big, warm palms. "A literal work of art. Beautiful. Intricate. Inspiring. Oh, and the tattoos are cool too."

Hiccupping and grinning, I pull his boxers down— and gasp. "Wow. And I mean a good wow."

Actually, "wow" understates the size and perfection of Mr. Suck & Lick. A mere wow doesn't usually make my pelvic muscles spasm in anticipation. Nor does it make my mouth water, not to mention my—

"Before we go any further," he says, his words slightly slurred. "I've got a question."

"I'm clean and on the pill," I rattle out. "But we should use up the condoms I got on a BOGO sale—they've got an expiration date."

His lips arc sexily. "I'm also clean, and condoms, as in lots, sound great—particularly non-expired ones. But what I was actually going to ask was: do you really have nipples on your butt, or am I so horny I'm just hallucinating nipples where they aren't?"

"Not a hallucination. This is merely a wet dream." As seductively as I can, I glide my fingers over the hard tips of my pierced nipples.

Gunther's pupils dilate, and a low growl vibrates in his chest. In an eyeblink, my back hits the mattress—making the room spin so fast time speeds up again. When I come to, my right nipple is in Gunther's mouth, while the other is between his fingers.

Oh, my. I usually need to explain to a nipple-piercing rookie what to do, but he's a natural. He licks, sucks, and (safely) nibbles just as he gently applies pressure with his fingers on the other side—all without the hard pinching or pulling that can be a problem with the piercings.

I realize I'm moaning from nipple play, something that's never happened before. Not while awake, anyway.

Is it possible I'm not fully awake now? It would explain the fuzziness that permeates my thinking. Whatever this is, I'm going to enjoy it.

In a moment of clarity, a revelation occurs to me—Gunther has nipples too. Great. I start to play with them, flicking and pinching until they become as erect as Mr. Suck & Lick.

Gunther releases my nipple long enough to grunt. Then he confidently slides his tongue down my belly.

I don't mean to overuse the word, but *wow*. His exquisitely skilled tongue laps around my belly-button ring and then continues its odyssey farther down, until it's exactly where I want it.

My hands grab onto Gunther's hair, mussing the slicked-back do.

I feel him smirk smugly against codename Pot, and then his clever tongue glides a circle around the stud in my clit.

"Fuuuuck," I gasp.

He stops what he's doing and looks up at me with a molten gaze. "Language, please."

"Sorry," I say demurely. *This* is how he should've motivated me to use ladylike words from the start. Pop into my office, get under my desk on his knees—there wouldn't ever be a single f-bomb.

Gunther resumes his all-important work.

His warm tongue becomes the center of my world, and then I break into pieces from a toe-curling orgasm—the only time it's ever happened so quickly. That is, assuming it was quick, and time wasn't playing tricks on me again.

Gunther doesn't relent, however. Softening his tongue, he makes his circles wider, which momentarily puts me back together again. But very soon, he coaxes another orgasm out of me, and I cry out so loudly my throat feels hoarse.

"Thoughts?" he asks, looking up with a crooked grin.

"I think two can play this game." I push him back and bend over him, ready to do what has always been implied by his beautiful cock's name: suck and lick.

Wow again.

The velvety skin is deliciously salty as I wrap my mouth around the steely hardness.

"Fuck," Gunther grunts gutturally.

I pull away. "Language!"

His smile is tormented. "New rule. Anything *fucking* goes in the *fucking* bedroom."

"Fucking yeah." I slide Mr. Suck & Lick back into my mouth, and just to highlight my point, I cup Gunther's balls with my hand, the heavy weight of them surprisingly pleasant to the touch.

Gunther's chiseled abs contract, and a chant of "fucking fuck" rushes out of his mouth.

Why does this make me feel so in control? No idea, but I enjoy the power trip as I pause the sucking momentarily. Then, when the object of my attention twitches in anticipation, I give it a couple of luxurious licks.

"I need to be inside you," Gunther groans.

"My favorite six words," I pant. Wait. Did that sound too slutty? In case it did, I add the truth, "To hear from you."

He looks around with great urgency. "There was mention of condoms."

Huh. My mind is so hazy—with horniness, no doubt—that I completely forgot. Feeling him inside me with bare skin is *really* tempting, but since my slut status was so recently under question, I decide to play it safe by locating the condom and handing it to him. Yes, I've basically slut-shamed myself to the point of resisting the very strong urge to put that condom on him with my mouth—a move I've practiced on enough bananas to feed all the monkeys at the Bronx Zoo for a year.

Oh, well. Mr. Suck & Lick actually looks more enticing thanks to the reddish sheen provided by the condom.

"On all fours," Gunther orders hoarsely.

I comply and over my shoulder ask, "This is an excuse to see my butt-nipples again, isn't it?"

In answer, he moves his face right up to said tattoo, but not to examine it closely, as it turns out. Instead, he licks codename Pot from behind—his tongue performing a maneuver clever enough to beat the world's chess champion.

My mouth goes dry, and it's no wonder—all of my body's moisture is down where Gunther's tongue is.

Time tricks must be messing with my mind once again because I'm on the precipice of another orgasm—which is when Gunther swaps his tongue for Mr. Suck & Lick.

"Fuck!" we both exclaim. In my case, it's because the

stretching sends me over the edge, making me come so hard my knees and arms nearly give out. In his case, it's probably because Pot's walls are squeezing Mr. Suck & Lick for dear life as I come.

"You feel so good," Gunther groans and thrusts into me once. Twice. Three times.

Fucking fuck. Is that another orgasm coiling in my core? I thought two is the max—and that's only if you're super lucky.

Yep. It's building—and the fact that Gunther's thumbs are pressing into the nipple tattoos on my bottom only speeds this up because those spots are erogenous zones for me (hence the ink).

"Faster," I gasp.

Oh, shit. He must've been holding back all this time. Now he pistons into me like our lives depend on it, and the pressure on my tattoo nipples intensifies as he tightens his grip on my butt.

Desperate moans are wrenched out of my throat. The orgasm that's been building in me is approaching tsunami size and is on the verge of making landfall.

Gunther grunts loudly, and his cock impossibly hardens as he reaches his release.

Yes. Yes. Yes. I'm pushed over the cliff, coming so violently that my knees and arms give out.

This is insane.

I end up on my belly, in a heap of bliss.

"Are you okay?" Gunther murmurs, stroking my back.

"I'm much, much better than okay," I say sleepily. "Now shut up. Please."

Chuckling, he wraps his body around me like a muscle Snuggie blanket.

All right. It's official. This must've been a dream, and that means it's time to get back to a dreamless slumber—which is what I promptly do.

Eighteen

I WAKE UP, ONLY TO REGRET IT IMMEDIATELY AND immensely.

The world is spinning like a NASA training module, and my skull feels like a dried-up tree being pecked by thirsty-for-iced-tea woodpeckers of Long Island.

Did I drink enough alcohol to feel this shitty?

I peek through my eyelashes. Oh, fuck. There's proof that I drank plenty—and also that what happened between and Gunther and me wasn't a dream, as some part of me was hoping. There he is, deliciously naked and *in my bed.*

I shut my eyes and attempt the impossible—a semblance of a coherent thought.

Here goes.

Gunther and I had sex.

No. We had mind-blowing sex.

Correction: it was ruin-me-for-other-men sex.

Unless... dare I hope it was merely mediocre,

but the alcohol made it seem like it was the best I've ever had? If beer goggles make homely dudes look hot, maybe Long Island iced tea goggles do this?

Wait. I'm focusing on the wrong thing.

I slept with the man who ruined my life.

Hold on. That's outdated info. Given what his father told me last night, that honor belongs to Tiffany —and there's not enough Long Island iced teas in the world to make me sleep with her.

Still, Gunther blackmailed me into working for him. Which reminds me: I'm HR's worst nightmare— an employee in bed with the boss.

Suddenly, a horrific sound rings out—one that feels like cat claws scratching on the pain center of my brain.

I peek at the alarm clock.

8:15 a.m.

Shit. I've overslept Bunny's breakfast by fifteen minutes—and this is just how his meowing sounds to my hungover brain. Come to think of it, did I feed him last night? Nope. I was too hungry for Gunther to do my fur-parent duty.

Gunther covers his ears with his palms. "For the love of all that is holy, please make it stop."

"On it." I slide my wobbly legs off the bed and wait for the room to stop spinning. "Don't look," I say to Gunther before I stand up.

"Isn't it a little late for that?" he grumbles, but he looks away.

Okay, so that proves he also remembers what we did last night. Peachy.

I put on my skull-patterned kimono that I got for free from the loyalty program of a punk-paraphernalia website. Sliding my feet into the slippers I also got free for referring my sisters to a shoe store, I step out of the bedroom—and am confronted by the grumpy face of my starving cat.

Do you know WHY I call you It-that-feeds-me? Or why I might rename you to It-that-used-to-have-eyeballs?

"Sorry, bud," I say and rush to the kitchen to open double his usual amount of food.

With a swish of the little bunny tail that is the signature of his breed, Bunny devours his food with uncharacteristic swiftness, making me feel so guilty that I give him another serving.

He looks at me with a little less grump in his gaze when I set down the extra portion.

That is smart. Maybe I'll let you keep your stupid eyes. It would be a bother to have to torture and kill one of those seeing-eye dogs.

To finish cat care, I refresh Bunny's water. Then I pour some of the same into two tall glasses and add in a little salt and sugar, followed by a splash of lemon juice. Finally, I fish out a bottle of pills from my medicine cabinet, and I take that and the two drinks back to the bedroom.

To my disappointment, Gunther is already dressed when I return.

"Here." I thrust a glass into his hand.

THE LOVE DEAL

After he takes the drink, I set mine on the nightstand, open the pill bottle, and hand him two pills, then swallow two myself.

"What is this?" he asks.

I gesture at the drink. "A cheap alternative to Gatorade." Setting the pills down, I add, "And CVS brand acetaminophen, which is the same thing as Tylenol but much cheaper."

"A hangover cure that's also a deal?" He grins—which makes him wince. "Thank you." He takes the pills and downs his drink.

"You're welcome." I drink mine slowly—because I don't know what to say afterward.

"We need to talk," Gunther says just as I finish.

Isn't it usually guys who dread that sentence from a woman? My heart sinks as I put down my glass. "Talk?" I look meaningfully at the bed. "What about?"

He rubs his scruffy jaw. "I'm sorry about last night."

"Excuse me?" My hands instinctively go to my hips. "You're *sorry*?"

He grimaces. "Alcohol was a mitigating factor. It lowers the activity in the prefrontal cortex, so rationality and decision-making suffer."

I narrow my eyes. "Whose lack of rationality and poor decision-making are we talking about?"

Hint: there is no right answer to this question.

"Mine," he says.

I step right up to him and poke a finger into his stupidly hard chest. "Being with me is a fucking honor,

185

and I'll be damned if someone acts like it was some kind of a mistake."

He sighs and takes a step back. "You're twisting my words."

"Am I? Really? Mr. Mistake."

"I'm your boss, which makes for an unhealthy power dynamic."

Why does him calling it unhealthy make it sound hotter? "You're just temporarily my boss."

"But that's not an excuse. Nor is alcohol." He sits on the edge of the bed. "I take full responsibility for what happened and am willing to work with HR. They have training and—"

"Shut up," I say sternly. "You didn't pressure me into doing anything I didn't want."

"But the—"

"Do you like your balls attached to your body?" I ask as I take out my trusty butterfly knife, open it with a flourish, and make a slicing gesture—pantomiming cutting two avocadoes from a branch.

Gunther scoffs. "Wouldn't you faint at the sight of blood?"

"Damn it." I put the knife away. "This is why I never tell anyone about my secret."

"So…" He sighs again. "I think my point stands."

"And what point would that be?"

He frowns. "I'm not sure anymore."

"Then I accept your apology."

"No," he says firmly. "We shouldn't have been intimate outside of a proper, HR-approved relationship. And even if that had been in place, our first time shouldn't have been under the influence of alcohol."

I perch on the bed next to him. "I'm not sure I agree, especially about the latter."

He turns my way and arches a questioning eyebrow.

A stupid blush sneaks onto my cheeks. "Didn't you think the buzz enhanced... the experience?"

He shakes his head, then winces again. "I figured it was just that way with you."

He did? My blush spreads all the way down to my toes. Also, I feel guilty for first threatening his wonderful balls and then for possibly bruising his ego by not attributing the awesomeness of the sex to him. Well, I can fix the latter if I backpedal. "It was *obviously* both you and the buzz, but since it was the best I ever—"

He leaps to his feet, and I realize that his pants are tenting like an anaconda has crawled inside them. I gulp and look up. His gaze is scorching hot.

Huh. He wants *more*. With the hangover? Come to think of it, I wouldn't mind some too, despite the soreness.

"I don't think anything good will come from having this conversation right now," Gunther says, sounding as stiff as some parts of his anatomy.

"Oh?" I channel Sharon Stone from *Basic Instinct* as I cross and uncross my legs.

His pupils dilate as he stares at my makeshift show. "We have to sober up," he growls—and it sounds like he wants to convince himself more than me.

"Fine," I say and close my legs very firmly.

"Great." He turns reluctantly and walks slowly to the door.

"Wait. Let me walk you out," I say.

He waits with his posture stiff—as well as other things.

As I walk in front of him, I can't resist shaking my ass for all I'm worth. By the time we get to the door, his breathing seems heavier. Good.

"Talk at lunch on Monday?" I ask as I open the door.

With a curt nod, he hurries out of my apartment.

Turning on my heel, I go dress myself and wait for the hangover to subside before I call Pearl.

"Hi," she says. "How did the party go?"

"Congratulations," I say with a sigh. "You don't owe me cheese for a decade."

Pearl squeals in glee and then demands to know the details, so I oblige.

"So are the two of you together?" she asks in an overly excited tone.

"No idea. We're talking about it Monday at lunch."

"Well," she says, a bit calmer. "Do you want to be?"

Yes. No. "Maybe."

"You do."

I roll my eyes. "Why?"

"You don't want to be single at Gia's wedding," she says, and something in her tone puts me on high alert.

"Are you still with—"

"Don't say his name!" Pearl says.

"Wow. Voldemorted. It must have been bad."

After she tells me about her disaster of a former relationship, I offer to take her out to her favorite restaurant for brunch the next day.

"Really?" she says. "But they never have coupons."

"I have a respectable job," I remind her, and I don't mention something I just so happened to learn the other day: that her favorite place happens to have a Groupon for this Sunday's brunch.

———

The rest of the weekend is a blur, the only memorable thing being how much Pearl enjoys the exuberant cheese tray at our brunch.

The first part of Monday is also very quick—until Gunther and I get to the gym floor, that is. Because I know we have that chat at lunch looming, the workout feels longer than the uncut versions of the *Lord of the Rings* films—and as awkward as the most rabid fans of the same.

"So," I say when we're seated in the cafeteria and our food is ordered. "Ready to talk now?"

"Yeah. Sure." He adjusts his tie. "Now that the alcohol has left your system, I wanted to reiterate my apology as well as underscore the part about me taking responsibility if—"

"Nope," I say with a headshake. "Been there, talked

about that. What happened is what I wanted to happen, period. Can we discuss something more interesting?"

He cocks his head. "Okay. Would it be acceptable if I were to court you?"

My heart leaps, and a buzzy beehive takes up residence in my belly. With a nervous grin, I say, "Leave it to Mr. Ferguson to make dating sound like it will require formal attire and fancy silverware."

He grins back. "If you insist, we could wear pajamas and eat with sporks."

"In that case, yes."

"Great." He reaches under his seat and pulls out a large stack of papers that he slaps on the desk. "Fill this out. I already did mine."

Ah. Form 66669. Of course.

I skim the first sheet of paper.

This policy does not prevent development of romantic relationships between Munch & Crunch employees, but it strives to establish clear expectations on—

Boring. And lies. Just the existence of such a form must turn people off sex and relationships as readily as learning about gonorrhea did for me for a while—after a "friendly lesson" from Gia and "the birds and the bees talk" from my overeager-to-explain-the-nitty-gritty-details parents.

I skim faster until I get to:

Individuals in supervisory relationships are subject to more stringent requirements due to—

Whatever. I'm not a supervisor, so not my problem.

I'm about to move on to the bullet points that

describe the actual guidelines when Gunther says, "Let me know if you want a quick translation from HR-ese into plain English."

"Won't that be difficult for you?" I turn the form toward him. "Your default speech sounds a lot like this form."

"Hilarious." He points at the first bullet, which states:

During business hours and in all Munch & Crunch-owned properties, Munch & Crunch employees are to keep personal exchanges limited so that their colleagues are not distracted or offended, in an effort to maintain productivity.

"Don't talk about personal things when on the clock," Gunther translates.

I nod sagely. "So, if I wanted to tell you that I enjoyed that thing you did with your tongue, I'd have to wait until after work? Or after work and after we leave the building?"

His eyes darken with heat, but he moves his finger to the next bullet, and before I bother reading it, he translates: "Don't have conversations that will make other coworkers uncomfortable."

"Isn't that kind of covered by the 'no personal talk' point?" Also, does he have this memorized, or is he that quick at translating HR crap?

Gunther shakes his head. "Yesterday's party wasn't company time, but if we talk about the tongue thing in front of our coworkers, it will make them uncomfortable and thus isn't allowed."

"HR people sound like Victorian chaperones," I say with a faux pout. "What else?"

He moves his finger down one inch. "No physical contact on company premises."

"Is this cafeteria a company premise?"

"Correct."

"So… I can't do this?" I put my hand on his. "Or this?" I brush my fingers up his arm.

His gaze grows hooded, but he firmly shakes his head.

"What about something like this?" I slide my foot out of my shoe and gently massage his crotch with my big toe under the cover of the tablecloth.

Looking like he might explode at any second, Gunther manages to say, "Yes. That is a great example of what not to do."

"What about non-contact?" I lick my lips libidinously.

His nostrils flare. "I'm sure that's covered under another clause."

I sigh theatrically. "I guess we'll be spending a lot of time over at each other's places."

He sighs almost as deeply. "Whatever happens, it will have to wait until this form has been reviewed by Vera Chaste, our head of HR."

Chaste? No wonder she doesn't let anyone else get any.

I sign the form. "How long will it take Miss Chaste to rubber-stamp this thing?"

"It's Mrs. Chaste, and I don't know. She's on

maternity leave."

"So not so chaste after all?"

He gives me a chiding look. "Don't you think Vera has heard that kind of joke as much as you've heard jokes about *that* which bees produce?"

"Touché. But seriously, when is Mrs. Chaste back?"

He shrugs. "Company policy for maternity leave is twelve weeks. She started a few weeks ago."

I gape at him. "That's a couple of months."

He smirks. "I take your eagerness as a compliment."

I press my lips together. "I take your lack of eagerness as the opposite of a compliment."

Gunther glances at where my foot recently was. "There's no lack of eagerness, I assure you."

The waiter comes with the food so I don't get the chance to reply.

When we're alone again, I say, "So that's it? Everything has to be on hold?"

Gunther lifts his fork. "Only the physical things. We will still have these lunches, so we can get to know each other."

I pick up my knife with the wrong hand—on purpose. "This feels like being friend-zoned."

He stares at the knife disapprovingly. "You'd have to actually act friendly for that to be the case."

"Fine." My smile is plastic. "Let's get to know each other. I'll start. What's your favorite color?"

"Purple. What about you?"

I tell him it's black, and then we fire off questions at each other at an ever-increasing speed. Among other things, I learn that he never carries a proper wallet on him, that he has a collection of swords at his house, and —not surprisingly—that a bee is his favorite animal. As the conversation continues, I make a decision: I'll do my best to break his will so that we get physical again long before Mrs. Chaste comes back from her maternity leave. It's a matter of feminine pride.

When I take him to the wedding, I don't want to feel like I'm lying when I introduce him as my beau.

To that evil end, I call Pearl as soon as I get to my desk.

"Hey, sis," I say without preamble. "Want to go shopping today?"

"Sure. What for?"

"Office attire," I say and throw a furtive glance at Gunther's office.

"Huh," she says. "There must be a big sale. What kind do you need?"

With steely determination, I reply, "Slutty."

Nineteen

"Your cleavage has cleavage," is the first thing Pearl says when I come out of the dressing room.

"Good. How does *this* look?" I pretend to drop something on the floor and bend to pick it up.

Pearl whistles. "He'll be able to see all the way to your uvula."

I straighten. "Is it work appropriate?"

She frowns. "Barely."

"Great." I wave at the sales lady. "I'll take this."

———

The next day, I wear one of my new outfits to work, and as I walk ahead of Gunther at lunch, I "accidentally" knock a fork off a nearby table.

"Oops." I bend to pick it up, butt out toward my platonic-for-now boss.

Was that a pained grunt?

I place the fork back and turn to Gunther, eyes as innocent as I can make them. "Did you say something?"

Looking stiff, he shakes his head. "I know what you're doing."

I squeeze my breasts together to show off the cleavage afforded to me by the outfit and the push-up bra. "And what's that?"

"Something juvenile," he says and strides purposefully toward our table. I can't help but notice his gait is off, like some part of him is in the way.

A big part.

And yet, during the meal, Gunther keeps his cool annoyingly well—just asks more questions about me and seems to really care about my answers.

No kiss or hug when we depart, and no invitation to his house.

What an asshole!

———

At the gym the next day, Gunther comes in dressed in a sleeveless shirt—something he's never worn before.

Hmm. It's chest day today, and the shirt he so strategically chose makes me want to touch myself, especially when he does the bench press.

Damn it.

"I know what you're doing," I tell him after he does flies.

He smirks. "What's good for the goose is good for the gander."

I squint at him. "Just wait until you take a gander at what this goose is going to wear tomorrow."

––––––––

The next day my outfit is skimpier, and Gunther is clearly impacted by it, but he doesn't say anything and continues the whole "get to know each other" crap as if nothing were amiss. But on the following day, he retaliates by wearing short shorts at the gym—and on leg day no less.

Grr. The sight of those powerful thighs is etched in my mind for the rest of the workday, and resolving the issue takes a long and aggressive session with codename Pot, one involving my phone on maximum vibration, a condom, and a cucumber.

Things escalate from there. We each wear clothes and do things to turn the other on—a kind of arms race where, instead of a huge weapons arsenal, he ends up with blue balls and I with the lady equivalent. It gets so bad that by the time the day of the royal wedding comes around, I feel like my nipples might ejaculate something—especially when I watch Gunther working his triceps at the gym.

This is it. I'm ready to ask Blue for his address so I can sneak into his house at night—naked.

It's the logical next step.

But wait. What if he has bees guarding him at night?

Maybe I could do it on a rainy day? Do bees fly in the rain? I have no idea, but I know who will be happy to share this beekeeping knowledge—and so, at lunch, I ask him.

"Since when are you interested in bees?" he asks.

He's got a point there. I've been uninterested in his so-called hobby until now—maybe even avoided talking about it, mostly on account of the word "honey" inevitably popping up.

Oh, well. Since I can't exactly tell him about my prior train of thought, I resort to a lie that's not completely a lie: "Bees are important to you, so it makes them fair game in the whole get-to-know-you process."

Looking skeptical, he says, "Bees *can* fly in the rain, but they prefer not to. A collision with a raindrop will destabilize the flight of a bee, as well as make her heavier. It can also drop her body temperature—which isn't good. Bees like to forage when it's nice and sunny, so they can navigate better and so that the nectar and pollen don't get washed away by the rain."

"Poor bees," I say.

He nods. "The good news is that they can anticipate the weather and store pollen and nectar, so they can get by when it rains."

"Well, that's something." I wonder how many more bee facts I am in for now that I've opened this pandora's hive.

"If you don't mind, I'd like to change the subject," Gunther says, his expression turning serious.

I arch an incredulous eyebrow. "From bees?" That would be like Pearl not talking about cheese, or bees not wanting to dance about the location of a juicy flower, or a skunk—

"Mrs. Chaste has come back," Gunther states.

I nearly drop my fork. "You mean—"

"As of today, our 66669s are approved." The scorching gaze he pins me with should be illegal. "So… we're free to do whatever we want."

An entire XXX-rated double feature plays out in front of my eyes as I consider all that is encapsulated in that "whatever we want."

"Assuming you're still up for it," he adds.

"Up for it?" I take a calming breath. "If it weren't for that stupid section in the form, I'd say let's sweep all this food off the table and—"

"The form is still going to be our guideline," he says, frowning. "Along with basic hygiene. And laws about public lewdness."

"Spoilsport. Tonight then. Your house." I give him a look that dares him to contradict.

"Sure," he says, but there's a hesitation in his voice, one that completely contradicts the hunger with which his gaze roams my decolletage.

I narrow my eyes at him. "What now?"

"Your sister's wedding is today," he reminds me.

I wave that away. "Obviously, we'll go after." As

much as I'm craving Mr. Suck & Lick, I wouldn't want to cross Gia on her wedding day.

"In that case, I have a condition," Gunther says.

I lower my voice. "We're both clean, and I'm still on the pill so condoms *are* optional."

No, that's not hunger in his gaze—it's starvation. "That's not what I meant."

"Consider it my condition then," I say, and blush like a goth virgin.

He nods and looks to be barely containing himself. "So long as you agree to mine."

"Telling me what it is would speed this up considerably."

"No alcohol." His voice lowers to a husky rumble. "I want your judgement uncompromised when you agree to all the dirty things I will do to you. I want your mind clear to fully experience it all, and I want your memory sharp to remember every orgasm the next day."

Have I just swallowed my tongue piercing? Is the stud in my clit vibrating spontaneously? I don't know, but something about the way Gunther said that makes me ready to come on the spot. All I'd need to do is cross my legs the right way and—

"Are we in agreement?" Gunther demands.

Oh. Right. I'm expected to answer. "Umm. Sure. No alcohol." For this event and for a decade after if he so desires—so long as I get "all the dirty things."

"Great." He cocks his head. "Now, do you know any interesting facts about tattoos?"

Wow. The completely unnecessary seduction continues? He must know this is a subject I care about almost as much as coupons. Almost against my will, the facts spew out of my mouth—like how tats on the collarbone, ribs, ankle, spine, and chest hurt the most, and ones on the knees, knuckles, feet, and elbows fade the fastest. I keep telling him all I know about my prickly hobby until I run out of both food and facts.

As we walk to the elevator, Gunther asks if I'm going to be a bridesmaid.

"No," I say. "Gia has a gaggle of friends, all magicians, who will have that honor."

"Why?"

Shrugging, I look for my ID card in order to open the doors, but weirdly, it's missing.

"Could you get that?" I ask Gunther. As he does, I answer his question. "Gia's trickster mind works in mysterious ways. My guess is, she didn't know which of us seven sisters to make the maid of honor, so she simply excluded us from the bridal party altogether. That or she plans to perform a magic trick as part of the ceremony and doesn't want laypeople too close."

We stop next to Gunther's office.

"Okay," he says, his emerald gaze dropping to my lips. His voice is a bit hoarse as he says, "See you tonight."

I only trust myself to nod before I slink into my office, the word "tonight" spinning in my head like a vinyl record by the Ramones—specifically *Road to Ruin*.

———

When I get home from work, a package is waiting for me.

Yep, it's the automated cat feeder I bought just for this occasion, one that will let me feed the beast at specific times or via an app on my phone.

As I open the box, Bunny's expression is grumpy-curious.

If that's the new It-that-feeds-me, what stops me from slicing the old model into sashimi?

I pour the kibble into the device and use my phone to make sure it can deliver food into his bowl.

Ah. You get to live—but henceforth, you'll be It-that-is-I.T.-for-it-that-feeds-me.

I set up a schedule to make sure the feeder dispenses food tonight and tomorrow morning, just in case, then fill Bunny's water fountain with enough water for a week before I start coloring my hair for the big event.

When I've achieved the right color, I carefully style it, put on my wedding attire, and work on my makeup.

Just as I finish, my phone dings.

Huh. The limo is here.

That's right. I get a limo ride, like the VIP attendee that I am.

I click-clack outside, and when I spot my ride, I whistle. There's a crest on the limo's door, the kind a medieval knight might put on his shield. Must be the prince's family crest.

Neat.

After I climb inside, I receive a text from Gunther:

What is the groom a prince of again?

Ah. So he must be in an identical car.

With a grin, I share what I know about Ruskovia, the small Eastern European country where Gia's fiancé is from—not that I know all that much.

I plan to visit soon, I say to finish the conversation. *The wedding favor is a free ticket to the capital.*

Gunther replies instantly, *You can't pass up a deal, can you?*

Before I can retort, my limo stops next to the hotel that is our destination, and I let Gunther know.

I'm right outside, he replies just as someone opens my door.

I expect to see Gunther, but it's the valets. At least I assume that's what these guys are, though they may be called porters. Just as during my first visit here, the male hotel staff wear ridiculous outfits that include capes, bicorns, and bright pantaloons.

How disappointing that this isn't Gunther.

As soon as I get out, I look around—and spot the man in question. A gasp escapes my lips as I take in his tux-clad glory. His shoulders look extra wide, his clean-shaven face extra angular, and his slicked-back hair even more tempting to muss.

He notices me too, and his emerald-green eyes smolder as he checks me out.

"Your hair," he exclaims as he approaches.

"Purple," I say with a grin. "As in, your favorite."

He shakes his head wonderingly. "You look magnificent."

I step toward him to inhale the yummy mixture of cologne, beeswax, and smoke. Rising on tiptoes, I let my lips brush his ear as I whisper, "You don't look so hideous yourself."

I'm pretty sure he shivers.

We turn toward the Palace, which, unimaginatively, looks like a palace. There's a mixture of different European architectural influences in the design, though mostly Russian and French.

Two pantalooned dudes open the doors for us, and Gunther gestures for me to go first. I sway my hips as I walk, a habit I picked up from taunting him in the office, and when I sneak a glance over my shoulder, I see Gunther's eyes glued to my ass.

Score.

Grinning furtively, I enter the giant lobby. Here too is a mix of European influences, like Russian-style icons and Italian frescos.

Then I spot something that makes my grin widen in schadenfreude: live birds, both in cages and walking free—as in, Blue's worst nightmare. How will she make it to this wedding? There are parrots here, which Blue considers equivalent to Stephen King's clowns. Also, peacocks—birds that the bride once told me were spelled "pee-cocks" because "pee comes from cocks, while peas and cocks have nothing in common."

"Let me escort you to the wedding," says one of the pantaloons.

"How does he know that's where we're headed?" Gunther whispers.

I shrug. "He may have escorted five other women with my exact face by now. That, or this whole hotel is dedicated to the wedding."

The second theory seems likelier with every step we take. The flower arrangements all around us include Gia's favorites, and hand-sanitizing stations are everywhere—something that wasn't the case the last time I was here.

"In here," the pantaloon says, gesturing at a door leading into a large theater. "But please, use Purell on your hands first."

When we step inside, I recognize the space—it's the very theater where Gia had her magic show. Is that what she's doing now? A show before her wedding?

"Thing 6," yells a familiar voice. "Over here."

"That's my dad," I explain to Gunther before he can ask. "He nicknamed us all Things one through eight."

Gunther grins. With a sigh, I scan the rows of seats.

Yep. There they all are. Mom and Dad, happy as clams to be giving away a daughter for the second time. All my grandparents are here too. They flew in from Florida with my sister Olive—a heroic act, given that our current weather is in the sixties, a.k.a. the bitterest cold for them. Most of my other sisters are here as well with their hot guys. Pearl, however, is missing— probably away on some cheese business—and the bride isn't here either. She's no doubt getting dressed for the big event. Oh, and Pixie's date seems to be Fabio, our old friend from high school who's always been exclusively interested in men.

"Namaste, sunshine." Mom gestures to the two seats next to her and Dad. "Why don't you sit here and introduce us to your date?"

I narrow my eyes at my clutch mates. It's super likely they left that spot available on purpose.

"Early bird gets the worm," Olive whispers as we pass her and her long-haired surfer-dude beaux.

Overhearing her, Blue cringes, making me wonder again how she got past those birds in the lobby. Working theory: her Ken-doll significant other put a blindfold on her and carried her over. He looks strong enough for the job.

"This is Gunther," I say to everyone but do my best to exclude Mom and Dad—because the chance of them saying something embarrassing is the highest.

"Nice to meet you," all my grandparents say in unison, as if they'd rehearsed it.

"I obviously already know Gunther," Fabio says with a grin before fist-bumping my date. "We all do."

"All?" Mom asks.

"Except maybe Holly." Fabio gestures at the non-bride half of the twins.

"Bollocks," Holly says. "I remember him too."

"You hear that?" Mom whispers into Dad's ear so loudly that some people turn to see if she's right in the head. "Honey's date is her high school sweetheart."

"Gunther," Dad says, eyebrows furrowing. "The name sounds familiar…"

Shit. The last thing I want is to drag up my high school troubles.

Fabio must be on the same wavelength because he says, "Gunther was on the football team, so you might remember him from the time you watched us play."

Ah, right. Fabio was on that same team. He'd always say, "If being in that locker room means chronic traumatic encephalopathy, it's worth it."

"Football team?" Mom goes all moon-eyed.

Another kink? She collects them.

A pantalooned guy interrupts my reply by walking over with a tray of champagne flutes. "Anyone care for a refreshment as you wait?"

"What are we waiting for again?" I ask no one in particular.

"Orientation," says the pantaloon.

"Sexual?" Fabio asks.

Pantaloon's left eye twitches. "You want the drinks or not?"

Everyone grabs the flutes except for Gunther and me.

When Fabio notices my hand is empty, he asks, "The drinks are free, right?"

"Obviously," the pantaloon says with a sigh.

Fabio looks at me pointedly. "Did you hear that... manuka?"

Has he forgotten that I pulled a knife on him the last time he used that nickname for me?

"Honey will be abstaining from alcohol today," Gunther says. "And so will—"

"By Cthulhu," Olive exclaims, eyes wide. "The deal addict would only refuse a free drink for one reason…"

Clapping her hands together, Mom jumps out of her seat. "Finally! I'm going to be a grandmother."

Twenty

EVERYONE STARTS TALKING AT THE SAME TIME. MOSTLY, it's a mix of congratulations and teasing.

"I'm not pregnant," I state. To punctuate my words, I push Mom back into her seat.

"Oh, I get it," Mom says. "She hasn't told Gunther yet."

At this, Gunther arches an eyebrow.

"That's not it," I growl. "I'd tell him if I were, but I'm just not."

"Yes, you are," Fabio says. "You heard Olive's epip-honey."

I turn on him. "You realize I'm very much in the mood to kill someone, right?"

Fabio looks nonplussed. "If honey-one here were to become a murderer, it would be you. In fact, committing a fel-honey might just *bee* your dest-honey."

Okay, *this* was why I pulled the knife on him, not the manuka stuff.

"You said you wouldn't do terrible puns today," Pixie says with a pout. "Not after I've told everyone you're my date."

"I said I wouldn't do it during the cerem-honey," Fabio says. "This is orientation." Turning to the pantaloon who, until now, has watched everything in horror, Fabio adds, "You know, honey-vesdropping is not polite."

Groaning, the pantaloon dude strides away.

"Can we get back to Thing 6's pregnancy?" Dad asks.

I resist the urge to bang my forehead against the seat in front of me. "There isn't one."

Dad turns to Gunther. "Have you given her orgasms?"

"Don't answer that," I tell Gunther.

Mom perks up. "For pigs, orgasms increase fertility by—"

"Mom," a bunch of my clutch mates say in unison. "You promised not to talk about Petunia."

Dad leans into Gunther's ear. "That's the pig my lovely wife brought to orgasm—to help with artificial insemination."

Weirdly, Gunther looks impressed instead of grossed out. "Are you also into animal husbandry?"

"Also?" Dad twirls the tip of his silver ponytail on his finger.

Gunther's sexy lips twist into a very kissable smile. "When not running a company, I'm a beekeeper."

Huh. Beekeeping is considered animal husbandry? Who knew?

"I'm the only one in the field," Mom says. "I'm a chick sexer."

Gunther nods respectfully—which might just be the oddest reaction I've ever seen to Mom's job. "That's when you identify female and male baby chickens?"

This time, Mom and Dad look impressed. "Few people know that," Mom says.

"Sounds like an interesting job," Gunther says with apparent sincerity. Turning to my dad, he asks, "What about your profession?"

A few of my clutch mates groan because they know what's coming.

"I'm a penetration tester," Dad says with relish.

"Which isn't as dirty as it sounds," Mom chimes in.

"Because I penetrate computer systems," Dad explains.

"As a job," Mom adds. "When it comes to penetrating me, it's more of a hobby."

"No." Dad sits up proudly. "Penetrating my wonderful wife is more of a calling. A passion."

Oh, boy. Grandpa—Mom's dad—looks ready to commit murder. In contrast, Dad's dad looks proud and ready to say something equally pukey about his wife.

Mom must notice the trouble brewing because she abandons that particular embarrassing topic and asks,

"So, Gunther, Honey—did you two like each other back in high school?"

A man on the big stage in front of us clears his throat into a live microphone, sparing us from having to navigate such a loaded question.

"Hello, all," he says pompously and adjusts the collar of his boring gray suit. "I'm Dasco, the Jester at Cezaroff Court."

Gunther and I exchange amused glances. This guy looks nothing like a jester. More like a bureaucrat or an accountant. Or a pedophile.

"Later today, some of you may have the great honor of coming within close proximity of the King and Queen," Dasco continues. "To that end, we've set up this orientation in order to instruct the wedding attendees on the proper etiquette during such an auspicious encounter."

Who are the 'we?' I doubt Gia had anything to do with this. She's pretty chill. Also, etiquette doesn't sound like the sort of thing I'd have a jester explain, but then again, what do I know about royalty?

"Let's start with the proper greeting," Dasco says. "Men shall bow, but only with their heads"—he demonstrates—"and women shall curtsy." He demonstrates this too, looking comical enough to make me wonder if he did take some jester classes after all.

"Surely, he jests," Fabio whispers under his breath.

We all shush him.

"The key thing," Dasco says in the meantime, "and I

can't emphasize this enough: *do not*, under any circumstances, touch the monarchs. This includes but is not limited to handshakes, hugs, and pats on the back." This last one he says with a notable shudder. "Even air kissing and waving is discouraged."

Huh. Sounds like the royals will really bond over this no-touch bit with Gia, our family germaphobe.

Dasco keeps listing what not to do, and the list is long, with highlights like: don't turn your backs on the royals, don't exit a room before they do, don't ask for autographs, don't sit until they sit, don't begin eating until they do, don't take pictures with them, and don't ask them personal questions—or questions of any kind. "In general," he concludes, "it's best not to speak to them unless spoken to."

Everyone in the room breaks out into hushed conversations. I bet they're having second thoughts about accepting the invite in the first place, as I am.

"Questions?" Dasco asks disapprovingly.

Mom's hand shoots up.

Oh, great.

Dasco points at her. "Yes?"

"What if the King is on my hall pass?" Why does she wink at Dad when she says that? "Or the Queen on my husband's?"

I hope she's trying to cover for the jester in the jokes department. They're about to be in-laws with the King and Queen, so sleeping with them would be a bad idea—even if touching were allowed.

The jester's bushy eyebrows furrow in a very non-jesterly way. "What's a hall pass?"

"Never mind," a bunch of my sisters say in unison.

Dasco's frown deepens. "Any other questions?"

Holly tentatively raises her hand.

Dasco points at her. "Yes."

"What shall we call them?"

The jester blushes—and looks a little bit more like his job description. "I'm so sorry I didn't cover that. If you only speak English—as most of you do—you will address the King or any of his sons as 'Your Royal Highness,' and you will call the Queen 'Your Majesty.'" He looks around. "More questions?"

No one else raises a hand.

"In that case, everyone except the bride's family should proceed to the ceremony."

Crap. Does he know my family enough to realize we need an extra lecture?

"I'll take you to the Gallery," Dasco says when everyone is gone. "A family portrait is a Cezaroff family tradition."

This is when it truly hits me. I'm going to be related to royalty. Me, a woman who's never bought a can of soup without a coupon.

Gunther grabs my hand and gives it a little squeeze, instantly vanishing all thoughts from my head except for the ones about "all the dirty things" scheduled for after the wedding.

"In here," Dasco says, and I realize I've daydreamed the whole way to our destination.

When Fabio tries to step into the room, Dasco shakes his head. "Plus Ones aren't going to be in the portrait." He looks at Lemon's husband. "Husbands are allowed."

Lemon shows the maturity that comes with settling down into married life by sticking her tongue out at the rest of us.

"Sorry," I whisper to Gunther.

"Sorry you didn't marry him in time?" Mom asks.

I want to fall through the floor, a common occurrence when Mom opens her mouth.

"It's okay," Gunther says and nods at Fabio. "This will give us a chance to catch up."

I give Fabio a look that hopefully says, "Ruin tonight for me, and I'll rip out your balls through your nose and then make you sneeze."

Fabio winks, and the jester ushers me into the Gallery.

I can't help but sigh as we enter the museum-like room.

"Miss him already?" Mom asks. "Not that I can blame you."

I roll my eyes. "Is Pearl going to be here?"

Dasco wrinkles his nose. "Is that the one who's working as staff today?" He says "staff" with the tone I reserve for words like "filth."

I nod.

"In that case, no. But worry not, the royal painter will use the likeness of your other sisters to draw her—

just as he'll remove that metal from your face and make your hair human-colored."

I open my mouth to give him a piece of my mind, but at that moment, Gia and her prince waltz into the room, and everyone claps.

I grin. True to herself, Gia looks more like Morticia Addams than a bride at a Victorian wedding. Her groom is clad in some sort of military regalia and is dashing—as you'd expect a prince to be.

"Hi, all," Gia says. "Thank you so much for coming."

Like we had a choice. It was either this or evil pranks from her for years. Before anyone can reply to this effect, the door opens once more, and a horde of dudes strolls in, all with faces that look eerily like Gia's husband-to-be.

"Tigger," one of them exclaims when he sees the groom.

Ah. Right. That. I shake my head. If *my* name was Anatolio, I'd go by *that* name and never let anyone give me a nickname, especially one from *Winnie the Pooh*.

"Brothers," Tigger replies jovially. "Thanks for taking the time from your super-busy schedules."

Many of the princes reply in Ruskovian, which sounds vaguely like Russian.

The door opens again, and my family gapes at the newcomers, who at first glance look just like bears.

At second glance—and recalling Gia's stories—I process that they're dogs, but truly bear-like ones.

A few of the princes yell something friendly at the

bear-dogs, and the creatures wag their giant tails and run to who I assume are their owners.

Gia might've mentioned something about this. These dogs are to this family what direwolves are to the Starks in *Game of Thrones*. Let's just hope tonight doesn't turn out like the Red Wedding.

Lots of masculine laughter and barking ensue.

The bear-dog who runs to the groom is the weirdest of the bunch, on account of it wearing goggles, which combine with its coloring to make it look like a panda. Actually, a second dog runs to the groom as well, a much smaller one that's easy to miss behind the bears. It reminds me of a koala, which I realize isn't strictly speaking a *bear* bear. Both dogs show lots of love to the groom, and then Gia, to my utter shock, allows them to give her some doggy kisses —germs and all.

Blue follows my gaze and gasps in surprise. "Those are either the cleanest dogs in the history of zoonotic diseases, or love really does conquer all."

A new person walks cautiously into the room. Judging by the giant camera in his hand, I assume he's a photographer.

So this is going to be a photo, not a painting? Good. I get to reunite with Gunther that much sooner.

The sound of a trumpet interrupts everyone.

I turn.

One of the pantaloons is acting like an honest-to-goodness herald. When the trumpet noise ceases, two snooty people walk into the room, a man and a woman.

Everyone gapes, and on my end, I fight a smile because the woman reminds me of Cruella de Vil—which is worrisome with all the dogs around. This must be the Queen, or "Her Majesty" if we end up speaking, which I'd prefer to avoid. The King, a.k.a. "His Royal Highness" also reminds me of a Disney supervillain, even though he looks like all the princes—or more accurately, they look like him.

"Future in-laws!" my dad exclaims and sprints toward them, with Mom on his silver ponytail.

Is this going to be an international incident?

Yep. Before anyone can so much as blink, Dad is already hugging the Queen while Mom kisses the King on the cheek.

The royals look like they've stepped into sewage, and that's before my parents swap partners, and Mom shakes the Queen's hand while Dad jovially pats the King on the back.

Well, that no-touch policy is out the window.

"Let's go," Dad says and walks toward us, with his back totally to Highness and Majesty.

"How did you produce so many sons?" Mom asks the monarchs enviously. "Is there a secret position?"

It's like my parents are deliberately going down the jester's "don't" list, doing the opposite. Next, they will be asking for an autograph, sitting first, and eating before them.

Oh, and let's not forget we all are about to take a picture with them—which was also disallowed.

"My husband doesn't speak English," the Queen says.

Oh? Then why does he look so indignant after the secret position question?

"I was actually asking you," Mom says.

"My English is also so-so," the Queen says, with barely any accent. "Now, how about we begin the portrait?"

When no one objects, the Queen barks orders as to where everyone should stand—her sons around her and the King while the dogs are to be at their feet in the front, with us plebeians on the sides.

When everyone assumes their positions, the painter/photographer takes a bunch of photos. He assures us that he'll paint us at a later date and make us "look better" than we actually do.

"Like a human Instagram filter," Mom whispers.

Taking that impertinent comment as their cue, the royal personages skedaddle, which sucks for my parents because it robs them of yet another etiquette protocol they could've broken.

I exit the Gallery in time to see the King and Queen jump into two embroidered palanquins. Immediately, burly pantaloons grab the attached poles and carry them away.

Fancy.

Gia and Tigger share another, larger palanquin, but the rest of the princes stay with us.

Gunther comes up to me, his eyes gleaming. Stopping in front of me, he dips his head. "Would it sound corny if I told you I missed you?" he murmurs into my ear.

"I missed you too," I say, a bit too loudly as it turns out because a familiar voice says "aww" in a very sarcastic tone.

I turn and see Pearl. She's wearing a white coat and dragging a large cart behind her, one housing a barrel of cheese so big that even Godzilla would need to cut it into smaller pieces before munching on it.

"Looks like the cheese gig is going well," I say with a grin.

"Yep," Pearl says. "Sorry, but I have to run."

With that, she rushes down the corridor with her giant cheese—and, though it may be my imagination, one of the princes looks longingly after her. Or maybe after the cheese.

Dasco the Jester runs over to us, panting. "Come," he demands. "You're going to be late for the *obryad*."

He hurries down the corridor and we follow, though Mom and Dad grumble about not knowing what "*obryad*" is.

"In Russian, it means a ritual," Lemon's Latvian husband says.

"Or a rite," Holly's Russian date adds.

With a huff, Dasco speeds up.

When we turn a corner, an army of pantalooned dudes is waiting for us.

"Take the *orekhi*," Dasco demands.

"Nuts," Lemon's husband says.

Is he translating or talking about Dasco?

Must be translating, as it can't be a coincidence that the pantaloons give each of us a handful of nuts—specifically, pine nuts.

"Are we making pesto?" Lemon asks her hubby.

"No," Dasco says. "This is to throw on the bride and groom after the *obryad*."

Ah. So it's a bit like rice?

Nuts in hand, we are shepherded into a large hall where all the other guests are already mingling.

There's a big stage where a band would usually be, but right now, it's just Gia there, kneeling in front of the King and Queen.

"Is she being knighted?" I wonder out loud.

Dasco shakes his head. "When someone not of the royal blood wants to transcend, he or she has to ask the reigning monarch for permission."

Huh. What if they—

Gia says something in the Ruskovian language with such a heavy American accent that even I can hear it.

"No," the Queen says imperiously.

"*Nyet*," the King echoes.

Wow. Did they just snub my sister? Are they suicidal?

"I told Tigger to skip this bit," says one of the princes.

Gia leaps to her feet, annoyance on her face.

"My question was purely symbolic," she says. "But your objection is noted."

Translated from Gia speak, their objection has just landed them on her infamous shitlist—which means, among other things, that they now have to watch out for laxatives in their food and drinks.

Tigger jumps onto the podium and wraps his arm protectively around his bride. "The objection is rude and will be completely ignored," he says in a steely voice. "If you hadn't disinherited me already, I'd volunteer for it now."

Noses upturned, the King and Queen leave the stage—which is when the giant cheese barrel that Pearl was carting around is brought in, possibly to replace them.

Gunther leans in, his lips gently brushing my ear as he asks, "Is this some weird tradition that alludes to the King being the big cheese?"

I meet his emerald gaze with a grin. "Let's just hope it's not some bachelor-party-type situation where a naked hooker jumps out of the cheese."

A colorfully dressed priest steps up to the podium and chants something in Ruskovian.

"He says his name is Patriarch Fanta," Lemon's husband translates. "He will conduct the ceremony right now."

Fanta? He's not all that bubbly.

The Patriarch speaks for a while, but the translation Lemon's husband provides is short: "Do you, Gia, promise to obey your husband, and other sexist things?"

"*Da*," Gia says solemnly.

The Patriarch speaks for a shorter time, and I don't need the translation to know that he says, "Do you, Tigger, take this woman to do whatever you want with, and other sexist things?"

"I do," Tigger says in English.

The most bear-like of the royal dogs rushes to the stage, and I see a pillow with a box on its back.

I chuckle. Gia has a ring *bear* at her wedding, just like on *How I Met Your Mother*.

The Patriarch grabs the rings from the bear and hands them to the newlyweds.

Once the rings are on, all the princes and their countrymen yell, "*Gor'ko!*"

"I know this one," I whisper into Gunther's ear. "They yelled it at Lemon's wedding. It means bitter, but in this context, for some reason, it means 'kiss.'"

Gunther stares at my lips as though he's happy to *gor'ko* them right here and now. I swallow and look away. As much as I'd love to French him, hard, I wouldn't dare do it when it's Gia's moment to shine—because laxatives.

In the meantime, Gia and Tigger kiss, and it's so passionate the Patriarch blushes and scurries from the stage.

The princes yell something else at the couple, and one of them hands Tigger a two-handed saw.

What the hell? Is Gia going to perform an illusion now—cutting her groom into two?

Nope.

Gia grabs one end of the saw while Tigger grabs the other.

Are they about to—

Yep. They start to saw the cheese barrel as if it were a tree.

Back and forth they go, straining, before they finally finish.

I exhale a breath I was holding through the whole ordeal, and then I giggle as it hits me: Gia just cut the cheese. So did her new husband.

Seems like my sisters are on the same wavelength because they start to chuckle and snicker, especially once the surprisingly pungent smell of the cheese—or maybe feet—reaches our nostrils.

"It's an old tradition," says the prince who was eyeing Pearl. "The cutting of the big cheese is meant to symbolize the first challenge for a married couple."

"Yeah, sounds like marriage," Mom deadpans. "Day one, and he just cuts the cheese in front of you."

The laughter redoubles, and Gia joins in—which is good, because if she thought we were laughing at her and not with her, she'd unleash those laxatives all over again.

"Germans do something similar," the same prince says. "With wood."

"Ouch," Fabio says. "Here in America, we keep all sharp objects far, far away from our wood. Especially in the morning."

More merriment ensues.

"On the subject of wood," Fabio says when there's a lull in the laughter. "Is it time for the nuts?"

Another prince nods and tosses a handful of pine nuts at Tigger. With a grin, I join him, and so does everyone else. Soon, the stage is littered with nuts.

When we stop, Gunther leans in again, his proximity making me tingle. "Is it weird that this made me hungry?"

My stomach rumbles in reply. The last time I ate was with him, back at work.

"How about another *gor'ko?*" my dad yells at the newlyweds.

We all join the chant and keep it up until the cheese slayers kiss one more time and hurry off the stage.

The jester grabs the mic. "Everyone, please enjoy drinks and hors d'oeuvres as the Hall is being set up."

The bride and groom slink away while an army of servers descends on us with trays of food and alcohol.

"Are we still staying sober?" I ask Gunther as I watch all the yummy free drinks pass me by.

He nods, dark, heated promises in his eyes. "I want your mind clear."

Gulp. Can we leave already?

"Cheese?" Pearl asks, ambushing me with a tray.

I take a little toothpick with a piece of yellow, holey cheese on it and stick it in my mouth.

"Oh, my cheese," I exclaim after nearly swallowing my tongue in pleasure. "Did you put heroin in this or something?"

Pearl beams at me. "There are supposed to be rich

cheese connoisseurs here tonight, so I've pulled out all the stops."

I grab another orgasmic toothpick. "I think this would even impress someone who hates cheese."

Looking intrigued, Gunther grabs a sample of his own.

How does he make chewing look so hot?

"That's amazing," he says after he swallows. He pulls out his business card and places it on the tray. "If you want to sell your cheese at Munch & Crunch, please let me know."

Looking beyond pleased, Pearl thanks him and runs off.

"Good going," I say grumpily to Gunther. "Now I feel like a shitty sister for not thinking of selling her cheese at your store myself."

"I'll make it up to you later," he says huskily.

Seriously, when is the earliest polite time to leave a wedding?

The next tray has black caviar, so I check it out. The stuff is at least fifty bucks per ounce.

"You like?" Gunther asks after I finish my caviar cracker.

"It's salty and fishy," I say. "If I were to buy the stuff, I'd pay fifty cents per ounce, at most."

He grins. "You don't like slimy little black fish eggs? What a shocker."

I grin back and grab a fig with some yummy stuffing to cleanse my palate.

To my chagrin, Mom and Dad come over and start

asking questions about how we met. Gunther is a good sport, especially when Dad gives him an unsolicited shoulder rub. Still, when Dasco says it's time to head to the Hall, I'm relieved. My parents could've embarrassed me much more in that window of time.

Dasco leads everyone down a large corridor, and I can't help but overhear Mom loudly whisper to Dad, "Where is Gia and her new hubby?"

"I bet it's another royal tradition," Dad replies. "Consummating the marriage immediately."

"Yeah," Mom says. "I bet in the olden times, everyone in the court watched."

Having overheard, Gunther arches a questioning eyebrow.

I shrug. "It sounds like it *could* be true, but knowing Gia, she might just as easily be preparing for a magic show."

Our procession slows as we reach a table with little cards that explain where everyone is to sit.

Does it make me a bad daughter that I feel super-relieved Mom and Dad are to be at a different table?

Huh. Wait a second. Mom and Dad are sitting with the King and Queen?

Looks like Gia's revenge has already begun.

Twenty-One

BLUE, LEMON, AND HOLLY ARE AT OUR TABLE WITH their partners, along with one of the princes and a few other people I don't recognize.

"Hi," says a model-esque woman who's clearly here with the prince. "Which of you two speaks Russian? The guy?"

"Neither of us," Gunther says. "Unless she's been majorly holding out on me."

I shake my head. "No Russian here. Why do you ask?"

The woman flashes a perfect smile. "Every other couple at this table has at least one Russian speaker among them."

"Sorry to disappoint," I say. "I'm Honey, by the way."

"Bella Chortsky." She gestures at her prince. "This is Dragomir."

"Chortsky…" I look at Holly's date, Alex, questioningly.

"Yep. She's my sister," he says proudly.

"And mine," says another table neighbor, who could easily be Alex's twin. "I'm Vlad." He gestures at his pale, round-cheeked date. "And this is Fanny."

Fanny blushes like it's her job, and I'm not sure if this happens every time she is introduced to someone new, or every time she hears her man speak.

Vlad grabs a big bottle and nods at Gunther's shot glass. "Vodka?"

"No, thanks," Gunther says. "I'm staying dry today."

Vlad looks at me.

"Sorry," I say. "I'm also not drinking."

"And before you ask," Lemon chimes in. "They're not pregnant."

"Thanks," I reply with an eyeroll. Turning to Bella, I say, "If not drinking vodka means we get exiled from the Russian table, I'll understand."

Bella grins. "No. Stay. Please."

So we stay and learn that at *this* table, the men "service" the women by pouring our drinks and placing our food on our plates—which sounds chauvinistic until Gunther does it for me and I melt into a hungry little puddle.

Soon, Gunther and I watch everyone down a shot, and then another because apparently, Russians believe the break between shots one and two needs to be short.

"Would you like to hear a Russian joke?" Bella asks after shot number three.

Gunther nods, and I follow his lead.

"Vovochka is in math class," Bella says. "The teacher

goes: 'You have a hundred rubles, and you ask your father for a hundred more. How many do you now have?'" Bella pauses for drama. "'A hundred rubles,' Vovochka says. 'No,' the teacher replies, 'You don't know math very well.' Vovochka shakes his head. "It's you who doesn't know my father very well.'"

Everyone chuckles.

"Can I share the one you told me yesterday?" Fanny asks Vlad.

He smiles. "Sure, Fannychka."

"'Dad, congrats,' Vovochka says to his dad." Fanny arches her nice eyebrows theatrically. "'Explain,' Dad says. Vovochka smiles. 'Remember when you said you'd give me a hundred rubles if I passed fifth grade? I saved you the money.'"

Everyone laughs, which seems to provide an excuse for the Russian table to spend a while longer telling us more jokes about this fictional Vovochka kid. The torrent of jokes is eventually interrupted by Dasco, who calls from the middle of the room, "If I may have everyone's attention, please!"

The room quiets down.

"The newlyweds have a surprise in store," Dasco announces. "Their first magical dance together as a married couple."

My sisters and I exchange a knowing glance. Since this is Gia we're talking about, the word "magical" wasn't in that sentence accidentally.

Yep. She and Tigger come out onto the dance floor, and as soon as the first notes of the tango play, her dress changes from black to white, then back again. A few moves later, Tigger's tuxedo jacket vanishes, followed by the shirt he's wearing underneath.

"I know the next trick," someone at the table says. "Watch his nipple."

Nipple? Is that—

Oh, shit. Gia waves her hand over her husband's chest, and his right nipple disappears, then reappears, followed by the clothing.

Everyone claps—which is when the couple's feet lift an inch off the floor, and the clapping turns into a standing ovation.

The music stops, and the newlyweds land. Gia takes a bow, grabs the mic, and says, "Everyone, please, to the dance floor!"

"Not so fast," our dad screams from his table, making the royal personages cringe. "You owe us *gor'ko!*"

This starts the chant that pressures Gia and Tigger to kiss again—not that they look like they mind.

When the kiss is over, they run to their podium-like table.

Gunther stands up and extends his hand to me. "A dance?"

Clutching the proffered hand, I leap to my feet. "For not letting me drink, you owe me all the dances."

Once we're on the dance floor, a song starts—and for some obscure reason, it's Marilyn Manson's cover of *Tainted Love*. Odd choice for a wedding, but hey, the song is slow, which means Gunther and I get close—

and as soon as we do, I feel Mr. Suck & Lick jut against my belly.

I rise on tiptoes and whisper into his ear, "Seems like I'm not the only one eager for the afterparty."

The pressure against my belly intensifies as he replies huskily, "I don't want wedding cake. I'm having your pussy for dessert."

Someone help me. I need a new pair of panties.

He nibbles on my ear.

Can ovaries explode?

"You're such a gorgeous couple," my mom slurs nearby, and her proximity tempers my libido enough to think thoughts.

"Thanks," I call in her direction, and then frown because Mom is barely standing on her two feet and her dance partner isn't Dad.

It's the Queen, looking as wasted as I am horny. Oh, and if that weren't enough, back at their table, Dad is sitting on the floor near the King's chair, massaging his royal feet.

Gunther's eyes widen as he follows my gaze. "Maybe he's gotten a new job?"

"I wish," I say. "Dad likes to offer foot rubs to anyone who'll listen. I just didn't expect 'His Royal Highness' to accept one—assuming what's happening is consensual."

"Your father's fingers are divine," the Queen slurs.

He massaged *her* too? "How much vodka did you all drink?"

Mom's eyebrows furrow comically as she comes

closer. "We played a traditional Ruskovian wedding drinking game." She hiccups. "I won."

Did she, though? Can a drinking game even have winners?

The song changes to a faster one, and I lead Gunther away before Mom or the Queen decide to puke on us.

"Wow," Gunther says.

He's right. Lemon's husband dances like a god—which makes sense, given that he's a famous ballet dancer.

"That's a hard act to follow," Gunther says, but he begins to move to the beat nevertheless.

Why did he have to say "hard?" Now it's *hard* for me to focus.

Oh, well. Let's see if I can twerk while sober.

I show Gunther my back, then thrust my booty into him. The feel of something steely against my left butt-cheek nipple is my first reward, with many more to follow.

The next song is a tango, similar to the one Gia performed her magic/first dance to. Turns out, complex choreography is easier sober, so Gunther and I manage to tango—but to claim that my mind is clear afterward would be a boldfaced lie.

I'm drunk on all the hormones coursing through my system. Drunk on Gunther's smile and the emerald-green sparkle in his eyes, on the bead of sweat rolling down his forehead and the feel of his hardness against my softness.

"Is that the wedding cake?" Gunther asks after a few more mind-blowing dances.

Yes! It is. I grab his hand and rush back to our table.

When the cake slices are distributed, I attack mine with as much enthusiasm as Lemon, our family's sweetest tooth. Unlike Lemon, I do not sprinkle said cake with sugar meant for the coffee cups.

Gunther's cake is half eaten when I finish mine and say, "Ready?"

He stuffs the remnants of the cake into his mouth and chews quickly. Belatedly, I realize that Gia is unlikely to check that we actually ate the dessert. Oh, well. The important thing is that it's now socially acceptable to depart. Hopefully.

"It was very nice to meet you," I say to the folks at the table.

Bella pouts. "You're leaving so soon?"

I grab Gunther's hand. "We have a long commute ahead of us. All the way to Jersey."

"I understand." Bella rummages in a large suitcase she's apparently kept under the table the whole time. She pulls out a box. "Please take your farewell gift before you go. Something to remember me by."

I accept the box gingerly because I don't like the expressions on the faces of the other women at the table. When I carefully open the box, I blink a few times—and wonder if the fumes from the vodka have somehow made me drunk after all.

The box contains a dildo.

A veiny one, blue and big—almost the size of Mr. Suck & Lick.

I look at Lemon, who runs a blog about masturbation and is therefore an expert on all things dildo. "Did you put her up to this?"

Lemon grins. "If your gift is what I think it is, Bella runs a company that makes them."

Before Gunther can look inside, I close the box shut. "Thanks, Bella."

"No problem," the dildo maker says. "If you email me your feedback on it, I'll send you more."

"Honey may do just that," Holly tells Bella with a knowing grin. "Deals are her prime numbers."

That's arguable, but I won't go into that, as that would delay our departure—and that's the last thing I want.

"Bye." I grab Gunther's hand and pull him out.

To my huge relief, there's a line of people saying goodbye to Gia and the groom, so we're not the first ones to skedaddle.

When it's our turn to speak, Gunther gushes about how much he enjoyed himself. I take it as a compliment because I was rubbing myself against him on the dance floor for the majority of the time.

"The tricks were amazing," I say when it's my turn.

Score. Gia beams with pride. My sisters can be easy to please when you know the right buttons to push.

Gunther pulls out an envelope. "A small contribution to your future."

Small? The thing is filled with bills.

Oh, well. I guess I'll be keeping my own, much thinner envelope—or giving it to Gunther.

We speed-walk out of the Hall and into the bird-infested lobby, where Gunther switches directions and heads toward the concierge—a rare member of the staff not wearing pantaloons.

"Where are you going?" I ask.

His gaze is heated when he turns my way. "I don't want to wait a whole car ride. This is a hotel. We can get a room."

Why didn't I think of this genius idea? This *is* a hotel.

"We'd like to get a room," Gunther tells the concierge.

The concierge frowns and taps the screen in front of him. "I'm afraid there are no rooms available. There's a private event going on and—"

"We're part of said event," I say. "I'm the bride's sister."

The concierge looks me over and nods. "You do look like her. Still, I'm afraid—"

"What seems to be the issue?" growls a new voice that turns out to belong to the prince who was eyeing Pearl earlier... or her cheese.

"Your Royal Highness," the concierge says reverently. "No issue at all. They want a room, and I've informed them we don't have any vacancies."

The prince's eyes narrow. "What about the smallest honeymoon suite?"

As the concierge taps on the screen, his hands

tremble. "Oh, my, that *is* available." He looks at us. "The rate is—"

"Not important," the prince says. "Given the unpleasant customer service experience they've just had, the room is on the house."

He owns this hotel? Or this whole island?

"That's too generous," Gunther says. "I'll pay for the room."

"No," I shock myself by saying. "You covered the gift; I'll cover the room." I take out my envelope and pull all the cash out.

That I don't ask if there's a family discount is a testament to how much I want this over with and Gunther naked.

The concierge looks the cash over with a stoic expression and mumbles, "That will not even remotely cover it."

Gunther takes out a credit card. "Put the rest on this."

"Unnecessary," the prince states, pushing away both my money and Gunther's card. He turns to the concierge. "Never mumble while on the job."

Wow. Talk about grouchy. I'm glad he's on our side today.

The prince hands us both a business card. "If you need anything else, please let me know." He gives the concierge a meaningful glance.

"Oh, I'm sure that will not be necessary," the concierge squeals. "I will take the best care of them."

I snatch the card anyway. The name on it is Kazimir Cezaroff.

"Thank you. We really appreciate it," Gunther says to Kazimir and the concierge.

"Yes, thank you," I say. "That was so nice of you."

I'm getting Gunther *and* the deal of the century. Somebody up there is really looking out for me.

"Don't mention it," Kazimir says and strides away, his posture as stiff as the dildo Bella gave me.

The concierge places a key on the desk in front of him. "Please take the elevator to the fourth floor." He points north.

We sprint to our destination, and as soon as the elevator doors slide shut, Gunther leans down to give me a scorching kiss.

An eyeblink of bliss later, the stupid doors open.

Grr.

We run down the hallway toward the door that matches the number on the key, and when we step inside, I scan the room in awe. If this is the smallest suite, the largest must be the size of the JFK airport. Even Gunther—who's much more used to opulence than I am—looks impressed.

"It's big," he says.

"Speaking of big things..." I drag Gunther by the hand through the enormous space until I locate a stadium-sized heart-shaped bed, covered in rose petals. "Show me yours, and I'll show you mine."

He takes his jacket off lightning fast, like he knows

the secret behind Gia's clothes-vanishing trick. The rest of him is revealed just as quickly, and soon, he stands there gloriously naked and potently aroused, every muscle gleaming in the soft, romantic light coming from the fake LED candles that adorn the bedroom.

My breathing speeds up as heat floods my lower body in anticipation.

"Your turn," he orders in a husky voice and sits on the edge of the bed with his rock-hard Mr. Suck & Lick twitching in anticipation.

He wants a show? All right. I take my phone out and put on the punk rock song I've always wanted to strip to—*Rebel Girl* by Bikini Kill.

As I take my clothes off to the beat, I head-bang, purple hair flying everywhere.

"Fuck," Gunther grunts, over and over, like a mantra, and that just improves an already amazing song.

When I'm completely naked, I grab a nearby chair, plop my butt on it, and cross and uncross my legs—again, to the beat.

"Fucking fuck," is the new chant Gunther starts in response, egging me on until the song finally stops.

Getting my hair out of my face, I gaze questioningly at Gunther, whose eyes are ravishing as they examine every inch of my skin with all its piercings and drawings.

"I've wanted you for so long," he says with feeling.

I cross my legs. "You had a funny way of showing

it." I uncross them. "All this time, all you had to do was just take what would've been gladly given."

He scoots toward the edge of the bed, his cock looking painfully hard. "I wanted this done right."

I cross my legs and frown—only partly in jest. "Did 'doing this right' include intentionally wearing skimpy clothing?"

He sits straighter. "I only did that to get back at you because you were tormenting me."

"You think *that* was torment?" Driven by a wicked inspiration, I bend over to the pile of my stuff and grab Bella's dubious gift. "Let me show you what the word really means."

I open the box and take out the blue dildo.

Gunther looks at his competition like it's a unicorn horn that's about to sprout the rest of its horsey self. "*That* is Bella's gift?"

"Shut up and watch," I say in my best seductress voice.

To illustrate my point, I slide the dildo down my chest until its head touches the piercing in my left nipple—which pebbles immediately.

Gunther's silence is so total and absolute that I can hear his jaw bones clenching and his cock hardening.

Smirking, I move the dildo to my right nipple, turning it into a pointy little rock.

Gunther's pupils widen to the size of dimes.

"This is what I could've been doing to you for weeks." I kiss the head of the dildo, then swirl my tongue around it.

Gunther's hands bunch up the sheets next to him, like he's trying to stop himself from losing it.

Let's see how much control he really has.

I ice-cream-lick the dildo.

There's a sound of sheets ripping.

Smiling with my eyes, I put the dildo into my mouth, as deep as I can, then do a few in and out motions.

Gunther's balls look tight and full—and like they might turn blue at any moment.

I take the dildo out of my mouth and spot a button on the bottom of the shaft. Curious, I press it—and the thing starts to vibrate like a thousand phones.

Nice. I bring the vibration near codename Pot to lightly touch the stud in my clit—and almost come on the spot.

Gunther leaps to his feet, eyes wild.

I move the vibration away for a moment. My pulse is uneven, but I manage to say semi-calmly, "Why are you up?"

With a groan that reminds me of a wounded beast, he collapses back onto the bed.

I turn off the vibration and tease my opening with the head of the dildo. "As you see, I *could* get myself off without you."

"Look," Gunther says hoarsely. "You win, okay."

I slide the dildo a hair's width inside me. "I win?"

"As in, you're right," he growls. "I should've had you in my bed as soon as you wanted me to, HR and propriety be damned."

Grinning triumphantly, I put the dildo aside and kneel on the carpet in front of the bed before locking eyes with him. "Say 'you're right' again."

"You're right." The expression in Gunther's eyes is animalistic and raw—and completely in contrast to his nicely slicked back hair. "You are *always* right."

"There, see?" I croon. "You may just get that pussy dessert you wanted… But first…" I take Mr. Suck & Lick in my mouth—and it feels so much better (and thicker and yummier) than a dildo.

Gunther groans something that sounds like, "You're right."

Every move I did with the dildo I now execute on Mr. Suck & Lick—and just as I taste the salty hint of precum, I stop. I must have him in me if it's the last thing I do.

"My turn." Gunther picks me up and splays me on the bed, like an all-you-can-eat buffet. "Or maybe I should say, your turn?" Gently, he kisses my inner thigh, and then he runs his tongue upward until he reaches the piecing in my clit.

I lean back, letting codename Pot unfurl for Gunther's clever tongue.

Like a starving man, he laps at my folds, murmuring something all the while. Hopefully, it's "you're right."

The vibration of his murmur and the warm texture of his tongue short-circuit something in my brain, and the orgasm that I was close to earlier crashes down onto my pleasure receptors—making me come all over Gunther's gorgeous face.

He looks up, and I find it ironic how hungry he still looks despite having "eaten" me just then. "I want to be inside you," he rasps.

I dampen my lips. "Remember my earlier condition?"

"Bareback?" His eyes gleam ravenously.

Nodding, I grab the back of his head and pull him toward me for a kiss that leaves my lips puffy and sore. At the same time, I do what I've been dreaming about all this time—slide Mr. Suck & Lick into me.

"Fuck," Gunther grunts.

I reply by grasping his glutes and guiding his first thrust.

"You feel so fucking amazing," he says on the second thrust.

My eyes begin to roll into the back of my head.

He thrusts into me again.

With superhuman effort, I manage to gasp, "You could've been doing this all this time."

"You're right." He thrusts into me harder. "You're so fucking right." Another thrust. And another. The rhythm deliciously picks up.

A moan is wrenched from my lips.

He nibbles on my neck before he grunts something scorching into my ear—and I think it's "you're right."

And oh, boy, was I right. That we missed so many opportunities to do this is a crime against nature.

Gunther's hands cradle my face gently, but his lips capture mine roughly.

Hungrily.

Fiercely.

My nails dig into his glutes as an avalanche of an orgasm begins an unrelenting slide somewhere in my core.

He pistons into me like a sexy jackhammer.

A desperate moan escapes from my lips into his.

He frees my mouth, allowing my next moan to escape into the world.

"That's right," he grunts. "Come for me."

Fuck. The avalanche of the orgasm reaches its peak —and I don't even care that avalanches usually travel from the peak to the foot of the mountain—that's how much pleasure I'm experiencing.

As codename Pot's walls pulse frantically around Mr. Suck & Lick, I feel an aftershock cresting into another orgasm.

My walls squeezing must be what brings Gunther over his edge—because I hear his guttural grunt and feel his release, which propels me to come once again.

He stops, panting, then kisses me sweetly on the cheek before he pulls out.

I lie there, eyes closed as I enjoy the hazy bliss of the aftermath. Eventually, I muster the strength to murmur, "That was absolutely amazing."

"You're right," Gunther says, repeating the words with an undertone of masculine pride. "But, of course, that was just the beginning."

I open my left eye. "Oh?"

Smirking, he slides off the bed to get the blue dildo. "I think you owe me another orgasm."

I open my right eye. "Do I?"

"Absofuckinglutely." He turns on the vibration on the dildo. "Or more like, I owe you another, for making you wait all this time while you've been *so* right."

I grin like a loon. "Okay. I'm ready to collect my debt and/or pay you back."

He lets the vibrating dildo retrace the steps I had it go through earlier: left nipple ring, right nipple ring, mouth, and then the stud in my clit.

"Fuck," I gasp as my toes curl, and I come once again. Having Gunther use a toy on me turns out to be a million times better than using it on myself.

"Good girl," he growls. "Now get on all fours."

Seriously? Why? Oh, wow. He's hard again. Must be from watching me with the toy.

Thanking the penis gods for this gift of a short refractory period, I get into the position required of me, and three things happen almost simultaneously: he enters me, slaps the nipple on my right butt cheek, and brings the still-vibrating dildo to my clit.

What the fuck? How am I coming so soon? But I am. With a scream too. He keeps thrusting, so I come again and again, like I'm trying to catch up on all the sex I've been deprived of.

Then, with a powerful, deep, final thrust, he comes for the second time—and I join him.

That's it, though. I fall face down on the bed, feeling like a lemon that's been turned into lemonade.

He cradles me in his arms. "Shower or sleep?"

"I don't have the energy to respond," I mutter.

With a grin, he carries me to the luxurious bathroom and washes me as if I were a doll, then towels me off.

"Careful," I murmur when he brings me back to the bed. "I could get used to this."

"Good," he says as he envelops me with his strong body. "Get used to it."

Oh, I intend to.

The goofy grin is still on my face as I sink into the deepest sleep of my life.

Twenty~Two

Is that coffee I smell? And eggs?

I open my eyes and find myself in bed alone.

After dressing, I stumble around in search of the smells.

"Hi, sleepy head," Gunther says when I locate him in the ginormous living room. "I got us some breakfast."

I scan the offerings on the table in front of him.

Yep. He got all my favorites. The only way he could make me happier is if he took off his pants again—but I'm sure that can be arranged after the food is gone.

"Hold that thought," I say over my stomach growling. "Got to wash up."

———

As I brush my teeth and make myself presentable, the implications of last night hit me for the first time.

Gunther and I really did it. We had sober sex after a proper, honest-to-goodness date.

Or, to put it another way, I'm dating Gunther. The guy who I mistakenly thought had ruined my life.

I sigh. I bet even if I hadn't learned that he's not the one who got me into all that trouble, I might've forgiven him after the third orgasm or so.

Could we actually work? Could Gunther and I be an item?

I think we could. Except... why am I feeling so uneasy?

As I stare at myself in the mirror, I finally puzzle it out. The issue is that I'm feeling things that are extremely premature for this stage of the relationship. Specifically, I feel light and giddy when I'm with him, or when I think of him. It's like I never want to spend a second without him.

Oh, no. This could be a huge problem.

Though he's admitted that I was right that we needed to hook up earlier, there is the fact that we didn't—and it's all on him. Is it unreasonable for me to feel somewhat insecure that he was able to resist my charms, such as they are? Doesn't that mean that I'm more into him than he is into me?

Gritting my teeth, I give my reflection a stern look. "Don't be a fucking idiot. You don't want a repeat of the Spike situation, do you?"

Yeah. A dose of reality is just what I need at this juncture—or else the next thing I know, I'll have "Gunther" tattooed on the insides of my eyelids, so that I can be reminded of him even when I close my eyes.

"Good talk," I tell my mirror self. "I'm going to let things progress reasonably this time."

Thus determined, I return to the scrumptiousness in the living room... and to breakfast.

Damn it. I didn't notice it earlier, but he's got a case of bedhead, and it looks amazing on him, all that thick dark hair in those unruly spikes. It makes me want to slick it all back the way he usually wears it, just so I can muss it again.

My stomach growls.

Gunther grins at me—which is when his phone rings.

He dismisses the call without looking.

I put a few goodies on my plate when his phone rings again.

With a frown, he looks at the screen. "It's Ashildr," he says. Ignoring the ringing, he checks something. "Before him, it was Samson from security. How odd."

I shrug. "Maybe you should take it?"

Nodding, he accepts the call. "Hi, Ashildr."

After a second, he says, "Slow down, please. Tell me what actually happened."

What's going on? Is Ashildr exsanguinating through his nose?

Gunther listens for a couple of seconds longer. He sounds annoyed as he says, "Yes."

Another second later, his lips press into a tight line. "It was?"

He listens intently before he demands, "Who?"

Whatever the answer is, he doesn't seem to like it one bit—and gives me a strange look.

"Based on what?" Gunther asks. He gives me another weird look as he listens to the answer, then angrily asks, "Are you saying what I think you're saying?"

Whatever the reply is, Gunther shakes his head vehemently. "Can't be. I refuse to believe it."

Ashildr's counter makes Gunther's eyes widen. "What?" he exclaims.

He listens to the next bit with a horrified expression. "I have no idea."

Whatever he hears next, it makes Gunther squeeze the phone to the point of cracking, and then he vehemently barks, "No!"

Ashildr replies with something, and Gunther nods to this approvingly. "You did good. Tell him to forget it even happened. I've got it from here." After Ashildr says something else, Gunther says, "Thanks for bringing this to my attention. Take care." With that, he hangs up and picks up his cup to take a slow sip, not meeting my gaze.

"Everything okay?" I ask, frowning.

Gunther doesn't answer.

My heartbeat speeds up, which is silly, as I have no reason to be nervous. "Seriously, Gunther, what happened?"

"Everything is fine," he says, but he does such a poor job of selling his words that my worry doubles.

"Something clearly isn't." I bite a muffin, but it tastes like cardboard. "What did Ashildr say?"

Gunther's eyes narrow. "Why are you so concerned?"

I lean back in my chair and examine Gunther's odd expression. It seems like he's trying to hide a rollercoaster of emotions behind a poker face but isn't good at it.

I take in a calming breath. "Shouldn't I be interested in something that concerns you? Or are we back to being nobodies to each other?"

"Fine." He pushes his plate away. "Ashildr told me that the coupons have disappeared." For whatever reason, he watches my reaction very closely.

My blood chills as I begin to understand what might be happening. "What coupons?"

"The big collection," he says. "Down in the basement."

He's talking about the place I thought of as my home planet. It sounds like it got robbed—and everyone instantly jumped on the "accuse the girl with the tattoos" train. And hey, I can't blame Ashildr or the head of security for something like that. After all, I did create those fraudulent coupons for their company, which led to this whole preventative project.

But that *Gunther* also thinks I could do something like that? After he was inside me?

This had better be a fucking misunderstanding.

Gritting my teeth, I ask, "Do you think I had something to do with those coupons disappearing?"

The stupid poker face is still in play as he asks, "Did you?"

I stare at him in disbelief.

He is accusing me of theft, just like that.

I guess I should be used to people thinking the worst of me—and maybe I even deserve it a little—but I didn't expect it from Gunther for some reason.

Not anymore.

Not for a while, anyway. Not since I started to develop feelings for him.

That last bit must be why this feels like getting stabbed in the heart.

Well, whatever feelings I imagined I was having, I'd better erase them because how can you care for someone who would insult you like this?

I swallow hard and push away the hurt, letting it be replaced by righteous anger. "I can't fucking believe this." I leap to my feet.

Gunther's eyes narrow further. "Why can't you just calmly answer the question?"

I wish I had a stack of coupons here so I could shove them up his fucking ass. "Go fuck yourself," I grit out. "And once you're done with that, fuck Ashildr and your head of security."

The poker face shows a crack. "Can you please calm down?"

"Don't tell me to fucking calm down!" I grab my unfinished muffin and toss it at his chest. "I can't believe you could accuse me of this after everything."

He stoically brushes the ruined muffin off his shirt. "Seriously, can you calm—"

I don't hear the rest because my frantic heartbeat pounds too loudly in my ears. "I quit! Both you and your fucking company."

He takes a step toward me. "Can you just—"

I back away. "I don't want to hear any more. Ever." I turn away so he can't see the treacherous moisture in my eyes.

"Hold on," he says, but I'm already sprinting out of the suite.

Shit. I think he's behind me. I feel eyes piercing into my back.

"Don't you dare follow me," I shout over my shoulder.

The feeling of eyes at my back goes away.

Still, just in case, I run down the corridor—and knock down someone in my way.

A familiar someone—Blue, my clutch mate.

"Hey, sis," she says worriedly as soon as we untangle. "What's wrong?"

I wipe my eyes. "Nothing. What are you doing here?"

She points at a nearby door with the bucket full of ice she is holding. "We knew how much vodka would be imbibed at such a wedding, so we booked a suite ahead of time. But back to the topic at hand—tell me what happened, now. You know I have ways of finding out for myself."

It's true. Having that NSA background gives her almost godlike snooping powers.

"Fine," I say, feeling proud of how little my voice cracks. "Walk with me and I'll tell you."

She pales. "Mind going through a back entrance?"

Why? Oh, right. The birds in the lobby.

"Whatever," I say. "Lead the way."

She does something on her phone—most likely to notify her date that her ice run has gotten delayed—and then she leads the way as I explain what happened.

"Something smells fishy here." Blue opens the secret exit door she's led me to, one with no birds in sight. "Why do they think it's you?"

I hold back angry screams and tears as I say, "I'm tainted by those fraudulent coupons, and Gunther never got over it, I guess."

"But why would you steal something like that right before going on a date with him? That's stupid."

I shrug bitterly as we exit onto the street. "Everyone knows how much I love coupons. Maybe they figured they're more important to me than Gunther is."

"Seeing you with him last night, I have doubts about that," she says.

"Forget what you saw," I say.

"I guess." Sighing, she points at a nearby car. "That's your ride."

"Thanks," I say with feeling.

"Don't mention it," she says. "Go home. Relax."

Nodding, I climb into the car and tell the driver to punch it.

A couple of minutes later, my phone rings.

It's Gunther.

I refuse the call.

He calls again.

I don't pick up.

He texts me:

Please talk to me.

I delete the text and turn off my phone.

Eventually, the car stops next to my apartment building.

When I stumble into my apartment, I feel so miserable even my homicidal cat seems to pick up on it. He rubs against my legs, something he never usually does.

It-that-feeds-me just needs to ask, and I'd be more than glad to put it out of its misery. I'd even fight my nature and make it quick and painless.

Twenty~Three

I CRY THE REST OF THE DAY, STOPPING ONLY TO FEED Bunny because no matter how depressed I am, I'm not suicidal.

The next morning, I'm not feeling any better, so the crying continues—now bolstered by ice cream consumption, petting the stuffing out of my disgruntled cat, and researching those teardrop tattoos that are so popular in prisons.

By Sunday evening, I'm calm enough to ask my smart speaker to play the Ramones—which lulls me to sleep.

When I wake up, I still feel tired, but knowing that I won't go to work today only makes me feel worse. Turns out, I liked what I was doing at Munch & Crunch—who knew? Maybe I could do what I did there for some other company? Or start a consulting business focusing on coupons?

Oh, who am I kidding? Gunther will no doubt make

certain I never work anywhere related to coupons again. In fact, I'll be lucky if he doesn't try to put me in jail.

Fuck. I've made the mistake of thinking of Gunther again. I shouldn't have done that. For the millionth time, all our wonderful workouts and lunches flit through my mind. And the wedding, which was the best date of my life. And of course, the mind-blowing sex—both drunk and sober. I know that "ruined for other men" is just an expression, but what if I am?

It was *that* good.

And yes, the rational side of me knows that the coupon theft was a favor from the universe. I got to find out what Gunther truly thinks of me before things between us developed further and I fell for him even more, but somehow, rationality fails to make me feel any better. If anything—

"Hey," my smart speaker suddenly says. "This is Blue. Why are you ignoring my calls?"

I narrow my eyes at the source of the voice. "How did you get there?"

"We have to talk."

"I just got up," I grumble. "Can I at least wash my face?"

"It's eleven," she says. "This is urgent."

It's eleven? I rush to the kitchen and pour food into Bunny's bowl.

It-that-feeds-me is really milking this whole moping thing at this point, and my patience is running out. In fact, one more strike, and I'll take its pinkie... to start with.

Moving faster, I dress myself, go through my morning routine, and chew on an untoasted bagel as I turn my phone back on.

Wow. A lot of messages from Gunther. I guess he *really* wanted to tell me off.

Ignoring all that, I videocall Blue.

"Finally," she says. "I can't believe I do all this sleuthing for you, and you ignore my calls and messages."

"What sleuthing?"

I would say Blue looks like a cat that has swallowed a canary, but even if she were a cat, she'd stay far, far away from members of the avian kingdom.

"You have to hear this first." She enables "share screen" mode, and I see her press "play" on some app on her computer.

A voice recording begins playing.

"Mr. Ferguson," I hear Ashildr's voice say. "I'm so sorry to bother you on the weekend, but Mr. Samson from security was trying to reach you and I intercepted his call. He discovered an incident during a routine security check that he thought you'd want to know about. At first, I thought it could wait, but when he told me what it is and mentioned wanting to get the police involved, I decided to get in touch with you immediately."

Blue pauses the recording.

"Oh, shit," I say to her. "You're showing me the other side of that fateful conversation between Gunther and Ashildr?"

"I am," she says.

"Why?"

"Keep listening," she says, clearly enjoying the chance to be mysterious.

I growl, and she resumes the recording.

"Slow down, please," Gunther says, just as he did in front of me in the hotel room. "Tell me what actually happened."

"The coupons are missing from storage," Ashildr says. "You know—the huge collection?"

"Yes," Gunther says, sounding annoyed.

"It was last accessed yesterday…"

"Wait a second," I shout.

Blue pauses. "Keep listening."

"Fine."

Blue resumes again.

"It was?" Gunther asks.

"Yes. And the reason I thought you'd want to know is because of the identity of the person whom Mr. Samson suspects."

"Seriously, what the hell?" I say, and Blue pauses things again.

"Why would that Samson guy accuse me?" I demand.

"It's easier if you listen," Blue says.

"Fine."

She resumes again.

"Who?" Gunther demands.

"Ms. Hyman," Ashildr says.

Lie. Why is he lying?

"Based on what?" Gunther asks.

Yeah! Thanks, Gunther.

Ashildr sounds apologetic as he says, "Her ID card was last used to gain access."

"What?" I exclaim.

Blue pauses the recording again. "He said your ID card—"

"I heard, but—"

"Where is your ID card?" Blue asks.

I run to my clothes from Friday to check, then recall that it was missing after lunch.

Odd.

"Missing?" Blue asks when I get back.

"Yes. You know something about it?"

"I'll explain after. I'm about to have a question of my own."

"I still say Gunther should not have believed this about me—ID card or not."

"That's why I think you need to keep listening," she says.

"Okay. Play the damn thing."

She does.

"Are you saying what I think you're saying?" Gunther asks. In his defense, the question sounds angry—like his first instinct *was* to defend me.

Ashildr's voice is small as he says, "I didn't want to believe it either, but it's probably her."

No! Even though I know Gunther is about to believe him, I can't help but wish he wouldn't.

"Can't be," Gunther says. "I refuse to believe it."

Yes. I recall him saying that. He wanted to believe in me. What the fuck else is on this recording?

Ashildr sighs. "There is more."

This had better be good.

"What?" Gunther asks.

"She also tricked Ms. Severina into creating a hundred-and-ten percent discount code for Buzz Beerin, one where we'd have to pay the customers for every transaction."

Fuck me.

I'm so screwed.

Blue pauses the recording again. "That right there. Does it make sense to you?"

I feel sick to my stomach. "Unfortunately, yes. Buzz Beerin is the brand of honey that Gunther makes himself."

"And did you create this coupon he's talking about?" she asks.

I pinch my temples. "When we were pranking each other, I was *going to* create a coupon like that, but then I thought it would be crossing the line, so I didn't. At least I thought I didn't. I mean, I swear I pressed 'undo' on the whole thing. But now that I think about it, that button was so close to 'save' that it's feasible I fucked up."

"Hold on," Blue says and switches from screen sharing mode so I can see her face. "When was this?"

I tell her, and she types away frantically. Then she smiles in triumph and shows me her screen once again.

A new app is on the screen, and on it is me, sitting at my desk, about to click "undo."

She clicks it.

"The camera is too far away to tell for sure, but I think that could've been 'save,'" Blue says.

Sadly, I agree. "What did Ashildr say next?" I ask, even though I can imagine.

Blue un-pauses the recording.

"To make matters worse," Ashildr continues. "That coupon went into effect today, and there was a huge scramble around the stores to cancel it. Meanwhile, we lost money. Why would she do this?"

Gunther sounds horrified as he says, "I have no idea."

Blue pauses again. "You can see how this looks bad, right? He forced you to work for him and all that, so in theory, you *could* want revenge…"

"Yes." I smack myself for even thinking about that fucking coupon. "Then again, I slept with him. What kind of revenge is that?"

"Keep listening," she says. "You might like the next bit."

I will?

She resumes.

"Well," Ashildr says. "We need to know how to proceed. Mr. Samson mentioned involving the authorities and—"

"No!" Gunther says vehemently.

Okay. So he didn't want me in trouble with the cops again. That's nice.

"I suspected you'd feel this way and told him not to do anything without consulting you," Ashildr continues.

"You did good," Gunther says. "Tell him to forget it even happened. I've got it from here."

"Understood," Ashildr says solemnly.

"Thanks for bringing this to my attention. Take care."

I stare at the screen until I see Blue's face again. Softly, she says, "Even after damning evidence, he was still giving you the benefit of the doubt."

I shake my head. "He accused me. All this shows is that he had every right to do so."

"But did he *actually* accuse you?"

Blue types away on her keyboard, and a moment later, I hear my last conversation with Gunther.

"Everything okay?" me-from-Saturday-morning asks. After a beat, she adds, "Seriously, Gunther, what happened?"

"Everything is fine," he says.

"Something clearly isn't. What did Ashildr say?"

There's a beat before Gunther asks, "Why are you so concerned?"

Shit. It's like I was trying to sound guilty.

"Shouldn't I be interested in something that concerns you? Or are we back to being nobodies to each other?"

"Fine." There's the sound of a plate being pushed away. "Ashildr told me that the coupons have disappeared."

Huh. He didn't even go into the Buzz Beerin part.

"What coupons?" my past self asks, and she/I sound defensive.

"The big collection," he says. "Down in the basement."

"Do you think I had something to do with those coupons disappearing?" At this point, the defensiveness is through the roof.

"Did you?" To my surprise, on the recording, he doesn't sound accusatory. More like confused.

"I can't fucking believe this," is my Saturday self's reply, and before I can relive the rest of it, Blue takes mercy on me and stops the recording.

I swallow, feeling sick once more. "So… there's a chance I overreacted."

"You think?" Blue asks with an eyeroll. "And he's been trying to talk—and hitting your voicemail."

"Shit." I bite my lip. "I need to fix this."

"Yeah, you do," Blue says. "And this should make it easier."

The screen changes, and I'm looking at my office once more, but this time, it's empty.

"This is Friday," Blue explains. "You and Gunther are at the gym, as always."

"Oh."

"Notice that." She hovers the cursor over something by my keyboard.

I squint. "That's my ID card. I must've left it on my desk."

"Yep. Keep watching."

I wait a minute that seems to last forever before everything clicks—because Tiffany appears on the screen.

"Don't you dare," I mutter as she looks around furtively before snatching my ID and slithering out of my office.

Blue's face is back. "Understand now?"

"It was her," I say stupidly. "I probably should've guessed."

"It's hard to think clearly when you're upset," Blue says gently.

I shake my head. "Did I tell you I found out that it was *her* who'd fucked me over back in high school? Not Gunther?"

"No, but I'm not surprised." The smile on Blue's face is impish as she adds, "You don't have to cut her this time around. I've already made her pay."

"You have?"

My sister nods. "She's going to get audited by the IRS the next time she files her taxes. Oh, and said taxes might be on the low end, since Gunther has already seen the video I've just shown you. I sent it to him as soon as I discovered it, and he promptly fired her."

So this is what she meant when she said fixing this will be easier than I thought. Gunther already knows I'm not guilty of stealing the coupons.

The problem is, I'm not sure it will help. I'm still responsible for the Buzz Beerin fiasco. Plus, he didn't actually accuse me, but I acted like an ass toward him anyway.

If I were him, I might find it hard to forgive me.

I jump to my feet. "I was an idiot."

"I wouldn't go that far," Blue says.

"I let my own issues color what happened."

"That you did."

"I have to run."

Blue waves. "Good luck."

I summon a car and frantically dress in a way that will hopefully make a guy more likely to forgive me, with lots of cleavage and leg showing.

I give the driver a huge tip to get me there fast—without a coupon or anything, which is an unthinkable-for-me indulgence.

When the car is flying through the streets, I call Gunther.

No reply.

That doesn't bode well.

I listen to one of his earlier messages at random.

"Hey, Honey. I'd really like to speak with you. Seems like your phone is turned off. When you get this, get in touch."

Fuck.

There are many more voicemails after that. I select one of the more recent ones.

"I really wish I could speak with you, not your machine," he says. "I guess it's really over." Click.

No. Nothing is over. Not if I can help it—even if it means groveling.

I call again.

Nope.

I text.

No reply.

Not good. Then again, what I have to say is more of a face-to-face conversation, anyway.

The car comes to a screeching stop, and I rush into the Munch & Crunch corporate headquarters.

"Hi," I tell the security guard. "I lost my ID, but—"

"Ms. Hyman?" The guard reaches for something inside his desk.

As I nod, I hope he doesn't pull out a gun or a taser.

He hands me my ID with a smile. "Looks like it's been found."

"Thanks."

I grab it, run for the elevator, and take it to the executive floor. As soon as the doors open, I dash for Gunther's office—but he's not there.

I check the time.

Ah. He must be at lunch.

I hurry to the cafeteria, and by the time I get to our usual table, I'm panting like a greyhound after a race.

The table is empty.

What the hell?

I rush back to our floor and unceremoniously burst into Ashildr's office.

"Where is he?" I demand.

Ashildr blinks at me. "Hello. We thought you took the day off."

"I'm not guilty," I blurt. "And I need to speak with Gunther about that. I ask again, where is he?"

Looking ready to bolt, Ashildr eyes the entrance to his office. "It's the beginning of the month."

"Is that supposed to explain anything?" I position my body in such a way that Ashildr won't be able to get past me without a tackle.

"He has high iron," Ashildr mutters. "So—"

All the blood drains from my face. Oh, God, *blood*. I recall Gunther telling me about this. He does a monthly blood draw.

"When is he due back?" I ask weakly. I feel dizzy just thinking about what's happening.

Ashildr shrugs. "He's just left. He also mentioned he might not come back to the office."

My skin is clammy and I feel faint, so it's a huge surprise to me when my mouth forms the words, "Where is the lab?"

"It's a blood bank."

What a terrible combination of words. What will they come up with next—torture supermarket? Putrid laundromat?

"Do you have the address?" I manage to ask.

Ashildr gives it to me, and I stumble out of the building. Once I reach the street, I head right for codename "just bank," not for a second stopping to think about what I'm going to do when I get there.

"You've arrived at your destination," my phone GPS informs me.

Great. What now? Maybe I could stay outside and wait to intercept Gunther when he leaves.

No. I have to talk to him *now*. As in, I'll have to brave it.

The problem is, though I've decided to go in, my feet stay put.

Must go in.

My feet stay welded to the ground.

An older man walks into the bank's door—and holds it open for me.

Fuck.

I scurry in before I can change my mind.

To my surprise, I'm not instantly faced with blood bags and other hideousness.

What a relief.

I walk up to the front desk person. "I'm here for my boyfriend."

Is her smile ghoulish?

"What's his name, hon?" she asks.

Is this a good time to mention how much I hate being called *hon*?

"Gunther Ferguson," I reply. "He's a regular here."

She gives me a onceover that seems to say, *Yes, I know the hottie in question, you lucky bitch.*

"Room 103," she says. "I'll buzz you in."

Feeling like I'm one of those too-stupid-to-live heroines in a horror flick, I walk through the door that leads into the blood bank's spooky inner sanctum. I mean, just bank's.

Okay. I'm in a corridor—and nothing scary is in sight. I force myself to take a step. Then another. To my relief, the first door I pass isn't see-through. Nor is the second one.

Great. With the atrocities hidden, I might actually make it.

I walk cautiously until I reach Room 103 and knock.

"Yes?" someone replies.

"Gunther, is that you?" I double-check, even though it sounds like him.

"Honey?" he calls out, sounding surprised.

Without replying, I open the door—which is when the sight of Gunther smashes into my retinas: a catheter in his arm and a bag full of blood on the other end.

As soon as the visual center of my brain processes the disturbing image, the rest of me shuts down.

———

I come to with a gasp, a strong stench of urine and vodka molesting my nostrils.

A woman in a lab coat is above me, with Gunther next to her.

Fuck. I swooned again—and got treated to the wonders of smelling salts, which contain ethanol and ammonia, a.k.a. the kind of stink that would've killed my sister Lemon.

"Are you okay?" Gunther asks worriedly.

I examine myself. "Nothing feels broken or even bruised." Except maybe my pride. Oh, and my heart feels a little worse for the wear—but that predates the swooning.

Gunther exhales a relieved breath. "You slid down the door on your way down, but I was still very worried."

A beehive awakens in my belly. He was worried about me, even though I haven't even started to explain myself.

I turn to the woman in the coat. "Can we please have some privacy?"

Nodding conspiratorially, she says that she'll be right outside if we need her and departs.

I scan my surroundings. Nothing scary is in sight. I dart a look at the crook of Gunther's arm. His work shirt's sleeve hides the spot where he probably has a Band-Aid. I exhale in relief.

"Now," Gunther says. "Can you explain why you would walk into a blood bank with your particular condition? That would be like me going to a peanut butter factory."

I bite my lip as I look up at him. "I needed to talk to you ASAP."

He sighs. "Sometimes the line between foolish and brave can get blurry."

I swing my legs off the bed. "I want to take full responsibility for that Buzz Beerin discount. I didn't create it with malicious intent, I promise. It was a mistake. I considered making it as a prank at first, but then I realized it was a stupid idea—only I clicked the wrong button by mistake without realizing."

He sits next to me and takes my hand. "It's totally fine. More than fine. One of the people who used the coupon is a big influencer on TikTok and posted a video with glowing praise. As of this morning, Buzz Beerin is sold out everywhere at regular price—and I'm considering franchising the brand."

"Wow." I've only partially processed what he's said. His nearness and my hand in his are turning my brain mushy—and having recently fainted doesn't help. "And you already know I wasn't behind the physical coupon heist."

He nods. "I'm so sorry if it sounded like I accused you back at the suite. The pieces didn't add up, and I was thrown. As soon as I got a chance to think about it, I was certain it was a misunderstanding. I know you well enough by now to be sure that you wouldn't do anything like that."

My heart is starting to match my brain in the mushiness department. "So... we're good?"

He squeezes my hand. "You tell me."

"I'm good. At least in that I'm *not* upset that you accused me—since you didn't, and since I looked guilty as sin."

He frowns. "Is there a 'but' in there somewhere? Are you upset for some other reason?"

"Not upset, exactly." Time to blur that line between foolish and brave once again. "I know you admitted I was right about that wait we had to endure before we hooked up—but it sucked that you were able to resist me."

He winces. "I'm sorry about that. The truth is, even back in high school, I always noticed you."

I gape at him. "You did?"

He nods again, eyes gleaming.

"I noticed you too." Me, along with the rest of my female classmates—and some male ones, and teachers, and cafeteria ladies, and probably some naughtier members of the PTA.

"I didn't know that," he says.

"Now you do, but please keep talking."

"Right. When we met again as adults, I felt like I was falling for you too hard, too fast. Our night together meant the world to me, but I wasn't sure that it wasn't just a drunken adventure for you. Even once we got to talking about dating for real, I couldn't tell if we were in the same boat, and I used the HR form as an excuse to let you catch up. I see now that doing so was a mistake—and, as I already reiterated, *you were right.*"

His admission has left me speechless, so much so he's beginning to look worried—which must be why I blurt out, "I didn't just fall for you. I love you."

Yep. I'm firmly in the foolish end of the brave scale now. My heart hammers as I await his reply. As soon as the words left my mouth, I felt the truth of them. *I love Gunther.* Really, truly love him. That's why it hurt so much when I thought we were over and why I now find myself in this terrifying kind of bank. But does he feel the same? Does he—

He cradles my face in his hands. "I love you too. I

273

was working up to telling you, but as usual, you got there first."

"You love me?" I feel floaty and light, like I might swoon again.

"I love you." His eyes shine like polished emeralds under a bright sun. "I love the way you fight and the way you make love. I love our lunches and our workouts. I even love your pranks—though I'm glad we're past that. I love your lips, your hair, every one of your piercings, every inch of your tattoos. Oh, fuck, do I love those tattoos. Honey…" He leans in. "Let's make a Gunther vs. Honey movie."

I moisten my lips, the lightheadedness transforming into an incandescent sort of joy. "With a soundtrack by the Ramones or Kenny G?"

"Both," he murmurs and crushes his lips to mine in a kiss to rival any song.

GUNTHER

I CRADLE THE KITTEN IN MY ARMS AS WE SIT ON MY living room couch. Soft and adorable, he tugs at something overprotective in my chest, and I can't believe I'm about to allow him to face the biggest danger of his short life.

I pet him and he purrs, melting my heart that much more.

A goofy smile twists my lips. When Honey first brought this ball of fur to me from her sister's place a few weeks ago, it was love at first sight—on my part anyway, though I like to think he reciprocates in his own feline way, especially during playing and petting sessions.

I learned a valuable lesson that day too. As fun as bees are, they have nothing on cats.

"Should we call the whole thing off?" I ask the purring creature.

He looks at me with his sleepy eyes.

If Honey were here, she'd probably translate his expression to something like:

Silly daddy, what are you mewing about? It was you who kicked the beehive in the first place.

"True," I say softly. "I was the one who asked Honey to move in with me, which always meant you'd have to meet your father."

And I hope this meeting won't be a Luke Skywalker-type of father-son reunion, where someone loses a paw. Oops, spoiler alert.

"I had to do it." I scratch under his chin. "She'd beat me every step of the way in our relationship, so I had to be the first when it came to 'let's move in together.'"

The purring intensifies.

Allow me to reiterate: silly daddy.

Yeah. Honey said she'd give me her answer on moving in after we see how the two cats react to each other—so a lot is riding on what's about to come.

So far, we've let them smell each other's stuff.

I hear the door unlocking.

"That must be her," I tell the kitten as I stand up and take him to the bedroom.

When I come back, Honey is there, a carrier in her hands. "Ready?"

As usual, seeing Honey takes my breath away and stirs my cock, or as she refers to it, Mr. Suck & Lick. This reaction goes all the way back to high school, though more recently, there's been a more euphoric quality to it—a giddy excitement that harkens to childhood, rather than teenage, years. Being with her is like tasting chocolate for the first time—or the substance that she shares her name with.

"Did you plug in the Feliway diffuser?" she asks.

I point at the wall.

"Okay, that should help."

I hope so. The thing is supposedly pacifying to cats.

"Okay." She lets Bunny out. "Let him acclimate."

We watch with grins on our faces because it takes her cat seconds to act like he owns the place.

"Ready for the next step?" she asks.

I answer in the affirmative, and we go down our checklist of "how to introduce cats."

"Here goes," I say as I put the little one on the carpet next to Bunny.

Honey and I hold our breaths, ready to intervene.

Without a second of hesitation, Bunny gives his son a lick.

"He'd better not be tasting him," I say, only half kidding.

Another lick.

"Wow," Honey says. "I think he's about to cuddle him."

It's true—and I wouldn't believe it if I weren't seeing it with my own two eyes. Unfathomably, Bunny is acting like a loving father, and the son is enjoying every second.

"Do you think Bunny knows this is his flesh and blood?" I ask as a smile tugs at my lips.

Honey's exquisite shoulders move up and down.

"I'll have to ask Pearl. She wanted to become a cat breeder before she settled on cheese."

My smile widens. "Everyone knows that cats and cheese are interchangeable."

"I know, right?" Honey's delectable lips pull up at the edges. "Cheese is famous for keeping mice away. And it's super fun to pet."

"Cheese is as independent as cats," I say. "Quiet too. Clean."

She shuts me up in my favorite way possible—with a kiss.

She tastes like strawberries, which I've told her, but also like clover honey. The latter is an observation I keep to myself.

When she pulls away, I ask, "Ready to call operation Bunny a success?"

She runs the stud in her tongue over her front teeth —a mannerism that has a similar effect on me as an overdose of Viagra. "Will you finally tell me the kitten's name?"

Great. Blackmail. For whatever reason, she thinks I'm bad at naming things and likes to tease me about it. She talked me out of my earlier idea for the name "Bee" on those grounds. She also mocked the name I suggested for her consulting firm. I still think Bunches of Coupons is clever, as in the cereal Honey Bunches of Oats. Nor do I think anything is wrong with my honey brand name, Buzz Beerin.

"Come on," she says, her smile as mischievous as it

is irresistible. "Just spit it out already. Unless you don't have one?"

"How do you feel about Bunny Junior?"

She snort-chuckles, and even *that* is sexy. "As in BJ for short?"

The mention of BJ further revs up my already-engaged libido. "We can call him Junior."

"How about Peanut instead?" She looks down at the cats with a grin. "It has a similar diminutive feel, but without making him sound like an entitled douche."

"Too long," I say. "What about Pea?"

"Too urine-y."

I sigh. "How about Pean?"

Her eyes widen. "Did you say peen?"

"Pean with an a," I counter. "It's a type of fur, and he's got fur."

"Still too phallic," she says. "And sounds like 'peon' too—and I'm talking menial worker, not golden shower."

You know what? Two can play this game. "Have you decided if maybe-Peanut is your son or grandson?"

"Grandson," she says without hesitation. "That's just how heredity works."

"So… my son is your grandson?" I crouch to give Peanut a scratch, then hesitantly do the same for Bunny to make sure he's not jealous. "How very Jerry Springer."

She chuckles as Bunny inexplicably purrs. "That's nothing. If we get married, I'll be his grandma and stepmom."

If? Despite her claims that my poker face sucks, I do my best not to show anything. The truth is, I fully intend to marry her, but I know she won't consider my proposal until we have lived together for a while. Hence, I'm glad Operation Bunny has been successful.

Speaking of which… "When are we getting your stuff?"

Her green eyes take on that slick-deal gleam. "I have a surprise." She leads me to the front door and opens it with a "Ta-da!"

My—or I should say "our"—front porch is littered with suitcases.

"Let me guess." I put my hand on her lower back, right between the two dimples that drive me insane. "The ride cost the same with or without the luggage, so you brought it in case everything went smoothly with the cats."

She gives me a sweet kiss that immediately generates a monster erection. "How is it that you know me so well already?" she coos as I try to discreetly adjust my pants.

Trying to ignore said erection, I help her get all the suitcases in. Meanwhile, the cats are acting even more cuddly together, even after maybe-Peanut paws playfully at his dad's face.

"I have a surprise for you also," I say when Honey's bags are dealt with.

She looks at my crotch. "Go on."

With a smirk, I roll up my sleeve and show her my very first tattoo—one that I got in secret.

She frowns at it. "A cigarette?"

"No." I capture her gaze. "I'll give you a hint. It's an homage."

She blinks at me in confusion. "An homage to lung cancer?"

"It's not a cigarette. It's a cannabis joint."

The blinking stops, and the corners of her eyes crinkle. "Did you want to commemorate a time when you got very, very high?"

"It's pot," I explain. "As in, *honey* pot." I glance down at the zipper of her jeans, behind which is the tastiest thing in the universe.

And... I'm hard again. Or rather, hard*er*.

She groans so loudly both cats look up. "If we spawn, you're not allowed to name the resulting creature, nor give it ideas for tattoos."

Little does she know, asking if she wants to start a family is also on the list of items I plan to ask her first —probably during the first dance at our wedding.

I'm not sure if she reacts to something that is reflected on my face, or if she likes my blunder of a tattoo more than she lets on, but she bites her lip in that unique way that I find irresistible. "How about a proper homage?"

Finally. Beast mode unleashed.

I sweep her into my arms, carry her to my bed, peel off her clothes, and spread her legs so the target of my homage is there for me to admire.

The piercing in her clit glints in the light.

I kiss it, worshipping it with everything I've got.

The cold of the metal contrasts with soft, vinyl-y warmth surrounding it, spiking my hunger.

Her grasping hands tunnel through my hair. I nibble around the metal stud, her moans my reward.

Before long, she comes with a cry—and the lush taste of her makes my balls draw up tight, my cock all but bursting.

"Ready?" I ask hoarsely as I position myself above her.

She nods.

I enter her—and as always, it's like arriving home after a year-long journey.

Every instinct in my body demands that I hammer into her, hard and fast, but I rein in my lust and move slowly, passionately, making sweet love to her. Claiming her. Showing her with my body all the wonderful things I have in store for her. Making sure—

With a moan, she comes again, making the object of my homage squeeze around me.

As I go over the edge, the world disappears, leaving just the two of us, joined together into a perfect being made of love and ecstasy.

It takes a while before I'm back to Earth, but finally, my breath slows enough for me to speak. Gathering her into my embrace, I hold her close and say softly, "Welcome to our home."

And as she sighs in contentment, I claim her lips in another kiss.

Sneak Peeks

Thank you for participating in Honey and Gunther's journey! If you're eager for more Misha Bell, check out *Puppy Love*!

Looking for more laugh-out-loud romcoms? Meet the Chortsky siblings in *Hard Stuff*:

- *Hard Code* – A geeky workplace romance following quirky QA tester Fanny Pack and her mysterious Russian boss, Vlad Chortsky
- *Hard Ware* – The hilarious story of Bella Chortsky, a sex toy developer, and Dragomir Lamian, a potential investor in her next big business venture
- *Hard Byte* – A fake date romcom featuring Holly, a prime-number-obsessed Anglophile who makes a deal with Alex Chortsky (a.k.a. the Devil) to save her dream project

For more quirky, irresistibly sweet leading ladies like Honey, try our stories following the Hyman sisters and their friends:

- *Royally Tricked* – A raunchy royal romance featuring daredevil prince Tigger and Gia Hyman, a germaphobic, movie-obsessed magician
- *Femme Fatale-ish* – A spy romcom starring aspiring femme fatale Blue Hyman and a sexy (possible) Russian agent
- *Of Octopuses and Men* – An enemies-to-lovers romcom about Olive, an octopus-obsessed marine biologist, and her sizzling hot (and infuriating) new boss
- *Sextuplet and the City* – A laugh-out-loud fake marriage romance about a dessert-loving secret blogger who falls for a hot, Latvian ballet dancer in need of a green card
- *Billionaire Grump* – A fake relationship romcom about a sharp-tongued aspiring botanist, a sexy, Ancient Rome-obsessed grump, and one fateful encounter in an elevator that goes hilariously wrong

We love receiving feedback from our readers, and we are always interested to know what you'd like to see in books to come. Want your favorite side character to have their own book? Mention it in a review! We take all suggestions into consideration, and if you sign up for our newsletter at www.mishabell.com, you'll be the first to know who will be featured next!

Misha Bell is a collaboration between husband-and-wife writing team, Dima Zales and Anna Zaires. When they're not making you bust a gut as Misha, Dima writes sci-fi and fantasy, and Anna writes dark and contemporary romance. Check out *Wall Street Titan* by Anna Zaires for more steamy billionaire hotness!

Turn the page to read previews from *Billionaire Grump* and *Sextuplet and the City*!

Excerpt from Billionaire Grump

BY MISHA BELL

Juno

When I'm late for a job interview and get stuck on an elevator with an annoyingly sexy, Ancient Rome-obsessed grump, the last thing I expect is for him to be the billionaire owner of the building. I also don't expect to almost kill him… accidentally, of course.

Sure, I don't get the plant care position I applied for, but I do receive an interesting offer.

Lucius needs to trick the public (and his grandma) into thinking he's in a relationship, and I need tuition money to get my botany degree. Our arrangement is mutually beneficial—that is, until I start catching feelings.

If being a cactus lover has taught me anything, it's that

if you get too close, there's a good chance you'll end up hurt.

Lucius
Post-elevator incident, I'm left with three things: my favorite water bottle full of pee, a life threatening allergic reaction, and paparazzi photos of my "girlfriend" and I that make my Gram the happiest woman alive.

Naturally, my next step is to blackmail—I mean, convince—this (admittedly cute) girl to pretend to date me. That way, my grandma stays happy, and as a bonus, I can keep the gold diggers at bay.

Unfortunately, my arch nemesis, a.k.a. biology, kicks in, and the whole "not getting physical" part of our agreement becomes increasingly hard to abide by. Worse yet, the longer I'm with Juno, the more my delicately crafted icy exterior melts away.

If I'm not careful, Juno will tear down my walls completely.

———

"Are you calling me stupid?" I snap. Anyone could have trouble with these damn buttons, not just a person with dyslexia.

He looks pointedly at the buttons. "Stupid is as stupid does."

I grind my teeth, painfully. "You're an asshole. And you've watched *Forrest Gump* one too many times."

His lips flatten. "That movie wasn't the origin of that saying. It's from Latin: *Stultus est sicut stultus facit.*"

I roll my eyes. "What kind of pretentious *stultus* quotes Latin?"

The steel in his eyes is so cold I bet my tongue would get stuck if I tried to lick his eyeball. "I don't know. Maybe the 'idiot' who happens to like everything related to Rome, including their numerals."

My jaw drops open. "You made this decision?" I wave toward the elevator buttons.

He nods.

Shit. He probably heard me earlier, which means I started the insults. In my defense, he did make an idiotic choice.

I exhale a frustrated breath. "If you're such an expert on Roman numerals, you could've told me which one to press."

He crosses his arms over his chest. "You didn't ask me."

My hackles rise again. "Ask you? You looked like you might bite my head off for just existing."

"That's because you delayed—"

The elevator jerks to a stop, and the lights around us dim.

We both stare at the doors.

They stay shut.

He turns to me and narrows his eyes accusingly. "What did you press now?"

"Me? How? I've been facing you. Unfortunately."

With an annoying headshake, he stalks toward the panel with the buttons, and I have to leap away before I get trampled.

"You probably pressed something earlier," he mutters. "Why else would we be stuck?"

Why is it illegal to choke people? Just a few seconds with my hands on his throat would be a calming exercise.

Instead, I glare at his back, which is blocking my view of what he's doing, if anything. "The poor elevator probably just committed suicide over these Roman numerals. It knew that when someone sees things like L and XL, they think of T-shirt sizes for Neanderthal types like you. And don't get me started on that XXX button, which is a clear reference to porn. It creates a hostile work env—"

"Can you shut up so I can get us out of this?" he snaps.

His words bring home the reality of our situation: it's been over a minute, and the doors are still closed.

Dear saguaro, am I really stuck here? With this guy? What about my interview?

"Silence, finally," he says with satisfaction and moves to the side, so I see him jam his finger at the "help" button.

"It's a miracle that's not in Latin," I can't help but say. "Or Klingon."

"Hello?" he says into the speaker under the button, his voice dripping with irritation.

No reply, not even static.

"Anyone there?" His annoyance is clearly rising to new heights. "I'm late for an important meeting."

"And I'm late for an interview," I chime in, in case it matters.

He pauses to arch a thick eyebrow at me. "An interview? For what position?"

I stand straighter. "I'm sure the likes of you don't realize this, but the plants in this building don't take care of themselves."

Wait. Have I said too much? Could he torpedo my interview—assuming this elevator snafu hasn't done it already? What does he do here, anyway—design ridiculous elevators? That can't be a full-time job, can it?

"A tree hugger," he mutters under his breath. "That tracks."

What an asshole. I've never hugged a tree in my life. I'm too busy talking to them.

He returns his scowling attention to the "help" button—though now I'm thinking it should've been labeled as "no help."

"Hello? Can you hear me?" he shouts. "Answer now, or you're fired."

I roll my eyes. "Is it a good idea to be a dick to the person who can save us?"

He blows out an audible breath. "It doesn't matter.

The button must be malfunctioning. They wouldn't dare ignore me."

I pull out my trusty phone, a nice and simple Nokia 3310. "Full of yourself much?"

He stares at my hands incredulously. "So that's why the elevator got stuck. It went through a time warp and transported us to 2008."

I frown at the lack of reception on my Nokia. "This version was released in 2017."

"It still looks dumber than a brain-dead crash test dummy." He proudly pulls an iPhone from his pocket. "*This* is what a phone should look like."

I scoff. "That's what constant distraction looks like. Anyway, if your iNotSoSmartPhone— trademarked—is so great, it should have some reception, right?"

He glances at his screen, but I can tell he already knows the truth: no reception for his darling either.

Still, I can't resist. "See? Your genius of a phone is just as useless. All it's good for is turning people into social-media-checking zombies."

He hides the device, like a protective parent. "On top of all your endearing qualities, you're a technophobe too?"

I debate throwing my Nokia at his head but decide it's not worth shelling out sixty-five bucks for a replacement. "Just because I don't want to be distracted doesn't mean I'm a technophobe."

"Actually, my phone is great at blocking out distractions." He puts the headphones back over his ears. "See?" He presses play, and I hear the faint riffs of heavy metal.

"Very mature," I mouth at him.

"Sorry," he says overly loudly. "I can't hear any distractions."

Fine. Whatever. At least he has good taste in music. My cactus and I are big fans of Metallica, which is what I think he's listening to.

I begin to pace back and forth.

I'm stuck, and I'm late. If this elevator jam doesn't resolve itself in the next minute or two, I can pretty much kiss the new job goodbye—and by extension, my tuition money. No tuition money means no botany degree, which has been my dream for the last few years.

By saguaro's juices, this sucks really bad.

I sneak a glance at the hottie—I mean, asshole.

What would he say about someone with dyslexia wanting a college degree? Probably that I'd need a university that uses coloring books. In truth, even coloring books wouldn't help that much—I can never stay inside those stupid lines.

I sigh and look away, increasingly worried. My dreams aside, what if the elevator stays stuck for a while?

The most immediate problem is my growing need to pee—but paradoxically, a longer-term worry will be finding liquids to drink.

I wonder… If you're thirsty enough, does your body reabsorb the water from the bladder? Also, could I

MacGyver a filter to reclaim the water in my urine with what I have on me? Maybe through cat hair?

I shiver, and only partially from the insane AC that's somehow reaching me even in here. In the short term, it would be so much better if it were hot instead of cold. I'd sweat out the liquids and not need to pee, though I guess I'd die of thirst sooner. I sneak an envious glance at the large stranger. I bet he has a bladder the size of a blimp. He also has a stainless-steel bottle that's probably filled with water that he likely won't share.

There's also the question of food. I don't have anything edible with me, apart from a can of cat food… and, theoretically, the cat herself.

No. I'd sooner eat this stranger than poor Atonic.

As if psychic, the stranger's stomach growls.

Crap. With this guy being so big and mean, he'd probably eat the cat. After that, he'd eat me… and not in a fun way.

I'm so, so screwed.

———

Order your copy of *Billionaire Grump* today!

Excerpt from Sextuplet and the City

BY MISHA BELL

What happens in Vegas stays in Vegas. Or does it?

Okay, let me explain. I broke into my crush's dressing room to sniff his tights (not in a pervy way, I swear!) and got busted while, um... you get the idea. He then kind of, sort of blackmailed me into agreeing to a fake green card marriage with him. But hey, I'm not complaining.

Next thing I know, we're on a flight to Vegas to make our friends and family think we had a crazy drunken night and, in the spur of the moment, tied the knot. Except... that's exactly what happens. (Thanks a lot, vodka.)

Considering that he's the most desirable ballet dancer in New York City and I'm a garage-dwelling secret blogger with a major sweet tooth, there's no way this marriage could ever become real. Not to mention my totally crazy family and my aversion to every smell under the sun—except his.

All I can hope for is to not fall in love with my husband. That shouldn't be too hard, right?

———

The ballet I'm watching is *Swan Lake*, and my crush's role is that of Prince Siegfried.

Damn it. I'm jealous of that crossbow he's holding. Given that my goal is to get this man out of my system, seeing him live might've been a step in the wrong direction.

His muscles—especially on his powerful legs—would make a statue of a Greek god weep in envy. His gleaming eyes are pure melted chocolate, and dark chocolate is also what his slicked-back hair reminds me of. His face is angelic, with cheekbones so sharp-edged they look like the hard layer of Crème Brûlée after you break it with a spoon. Oh, but all of that pales in comparison to the bulge in his pants—a feature of so many of my masturbation fantasies that I've even named the contents of it Mr. Big.

So, yeah. Seeing all this is the opposite of helpful—and if I activate the vibrating panties I'm currently wearing, it will make everything that much worse.

Originally, I put on the masturbatory panties because I figured this is my last chance at a ménage à moi with The Russian. If sniffing his tights works as intended, I'll have to resort to some other visual aid for visiting the bat cave—like *Magic Mike, 300,* or *Charlie and the Chocolate Factory.*

Then again, I shouldn't be selfish. This adventure would make for an amazing blog post. I don't usually get naughty in public, so this might be educational for my followers.

Yeah. I'll do it for them. It will be my last hurrah with The Russian—made that much more interesting because I'm seeing him live.

I scan the nicely dressed people sitting around me. The coast is clear. They're focusing on the spectacle in front of us, as they should.

I fish out the little remote that activates the vibration.

Last chance to change my mind.

Nope. The Russian flashes me the perfection that is his butt, with a gluteus maximus that I want to lick like rock candy.

I press the "on" button and grin as my underwear begins to vibrate.

It's DIY time.

Even at the lowest speed, my clit is instantly engorged, and I have to hope the electrical components inside this technological marvel are waterproof. Soon, I have to painfully bite my tongue to keep from moaning. Tchaikovsky's music is genius, but it wouldn't drown *that* out.

I had no idea it would be this hard to keep quiet.

Must be The Russian's hotness in action.

Panting, I turn off the device to give my clit a chance to cool off. If I get caught doing this, I'll be escorted out and banned for life for being the pervert that I am.

When I think I can stay quiet, I turn the thing back on again.

Nope. Just as The Russian performs a particularly mouthwatering *fouetté*, the desire to be vocal is back with a vengeance.

Fuck. Me.

Whoever designed these panties should win some sort of a prize. They do to my nether regions what the Swan theme song does to my ears, or The Russian to my eyes.

An orgasm of cosmic proportions builds inside me, and staying silent takes an effort of will I know I don't possess, so I turn everything off once again, for good this time.

Fucker. Now I'm just really frustrated and cranky.

As if to sharpen my frustration, the ballerina playing Princess Odette shows up.

Can you say "impossible standard of beauty?" Translucently thin on top, she looks like someone who's never tasted a croissant in her life, yet her legs are powerful and seem to go on and on.

I know, I know. My jealousy is as green as a St. Patrick's Day donut. In my defense, her character is supposed to be sweet, noble, and guileless. She, however, dances the part with seduction, like Odile, the evil black swan. Speaking of *Black Swan*, it's all too easy to imagine this woman stabbing someone with a shard of glass, the way Natalie Portman's character did in the movie.

That's it. Decided. Henceforth, this ballerina will be Black Swan in my mind.

As the ballet continues, I cringe each time The Russian touches Black Swan—which is often, especially during the *pas de deux*. In fact, things get so bad that when Princess Odette meets her sad end, I find it hard to empathize.

I'm just glad the show is over. Watching it live was definitely a mistake.

Fighting the exiting crowds, I make my way to the bathroom, where I lock my stall and climb on a toilet to hide my feet as per Blue's instructions for Operation Big Sniff. Her instructions are also why I'm wearing all black—dressy pants appropriate for the venue, a button-up shirt that's slightly too tight on me (I bought it a few pounds ago, so sue me), and a pair of ballet flats that have seen better days but are the fanciest shoes I can run in.

Taking out an earbud, I stick it into my ear and dial Blue.

"Hey, sis," she says. "The crowd is dispersing as we speak. Hold tight."

As I wait, Blue fills me in on all the juicy family gossip, making me wonder how she gathered all this information. No doubt using the same nefarious methods as Big Brother in the dystopian world of *1984*.

"The Latvian Elvis has just left the building," Blue finally says. "And I turned off the cameras in your way, so you can start the op."

"Thanks." I move to hop down from the toilet, but my foot slips and I headbutt the stall door.

Ouch. I see stars in my vision—shaped like urinal cakes.

Worse still, I hear a sploosh.

No! Please no.

Sadly, it's yes.

My phone is swimming in the toilet bowl. Yuck.

"Hey," Blue says in the earbud through crackling static. "Is everything o—"

The rest is an unintelligible hiss.

My poor phone is dead.

I debate fishing it out, as gross as that would be. I've heard you can stick these devices into rice to dry out, and they may resurrect themselves. In the end, I decide against it. The phone is so old it's a stretch to call it "smart." It's better off drowning in the toilet with some dignity, even though I'll have to skip about a hundred trips to Cinnabon to afford a replacement.

The question now is: should I call off the operation?

I no longer have Blue in my ear, but I *have* splurged on this ticket and I don't know when I'll be able to afford another one. Besides, I've gone through all the trouble of learning how to pick a lock, and Blue has done her part already.

All right, I'm going for it.

Taking in a calming breath, I sneak out of the stall.

No one is around.

Good.

As I creep to my destination, I'm glad I memorized the layout of this place instead of relying on the schematics on my phone.

The first lock in my way is easy to pick, and the second door isn't even locked.

When I get to the last corridor, I realize I'm jogging, and by the time I stop next to the door of what should be The Russian's changing room, I'm panting.

Yep. "Artjoms Skulme" is what the tag on the door says. I'm in the right place.

I take out the lockpicks, and the lock yields to my newfound skills without much fuss.

Heart hammering, I step inside. In the large mirror in front of me, I look frightened, like Blue would in a bird's nest. Even my shoulder-length hair appears frazzled and pale, the strawberry-blond of my strands more ashy blond in this light than anything close to red.

Chewing on my lip, I look around for the tights. I've made it this far, and I'm not leaving without completing the operation.

Hmm.

I don't see tights anywhere.

Just my luck. He's a neat freak.

Wait a sec... I see something. Not tights, but possibly even better. Although also a bit creepier if I think about it too deeply.

I hurry over to the chair on which I've spotted the

item—an article of clothing known in this industry as a dance belt.

Except it's not an actual belt.

Designed for ballet dancers with external genitals that can flop about during vigorous jumps, this undergarment looks suspiciously like a thong.

I fan myself.

Just picturing The Russian wearing this butt-floss without tights makes me want to re-enable my vibrating panties.

But no. No time for muffin buttering right now.

I pick up the thong—I mean, dance belt. It feels nice and soft to the touch.

Must be made of boyfriend material.

I peer at the dance belt like I'm trying to charm a snake inside of it. A snake named Mr. Big.

Am I really going to do this? And if I do, does that mean I'm like one of those peeps who buy worn underwear online?

No. I don't have an undies-sniffing fetish, more like the opposite.

Yeah. If anyone asks, that's my excuse.

With determined movements, I rip the filter from each nostril and bring the dance belt up to my nose.

Here goes.

I take the Big Sniff.

———

Order your copy of *Sextuplet and the City* today!

About the Author

We love writing humor (often the inappropriate kind), happy endings (both kinds), and characters quirky enough to be called oddballs (because… balls). If you love your romance heavy on the comedy and feel-good vibes, visit www.mishabell.com and sign up for our newsletter.